For my parents

The Silver Chain

JION SHEIBANI

HOT
KEY
BOOKS

First published in Great Britain in 2022 by
HOT KEY BOOKS
4th Floor, Victoria House, Bloomsbury Square
London WC1B 4DA
Owned by Bonnier Books
Sveavägen 56, Stockholm, Sweden
www.hotkeybooks.com

ISBN: 978-1-4714-1150-2
Also available as an ebook and audio

1

Typeset by Suzanne Cooper
Printed and bound in Great Britain

Hot Key Books is an imprint of Bonnier Books UK
www.bonnierbooks.co.uk

He rises and begins to round,
He drops the silver chain of sound
Of many links without a break,
In chirrup, whistle, slur and shake

'The Lark Ascending', George Meredith

Where it seems to start

It's the end of a long summer.
Mum's hanging out the washing in the backyard
and I'm next to her, in the deckchair,
wearing my padded bikini,
worrying about how teeny my boobs are.
I want to catch a tan before school starts
but she's gone and pegged the clothes

     way

           too

                  close

and they're flapping in my face,
blocking out my sun.

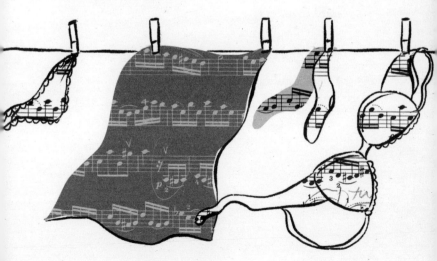

I'm writing my autobiography,
she suddenly says, dead confident,
like she's some kind of celebrity.

She's been having these manic days
and I know I should just say
        nothing
but that tea towel's whipping in the wind
and I snap.

Who on EARTH would want to read
YOUR autobiography?!

I see her mouth twitch.
I know I sound like a bitch
but I can't seem to stop.
I'm sick of bottling it all up
and pretending this person is her,
I'm sick of this version
of Mum stamping out
the old one.

She squeezes the pegs, clamps

more damp things

onto the line.

There's a lot you don't know about my life,
a lot of very interesting things, she says.
More interesting than that book of yours.

More interesting than Shakespeare?
Yeah, course! I scoff

and that's when it all kicks off.

She storms inside and slams the door
and I wish things back to before.

Before

Mum was
a secretary, a potter,
a big fat spider swatter,
a watercolour painter,
the best pancake maker,
a galaxy of hugs and kisses,
a fan of all Indian dishes,
a Pictionary winner,
a TikTok beginner,
brilliant at sewing,
always watching her plants growing,
the homework police,
complex, like a jigsaw piece,
an alarm clock,
a rock,
stable
like the bus timetable,
a Tina Turner dancer,
the one who always had The Answer.

Sorry

I say it through gritted teeth
but she still goes upstairs, curls underneath the sheets
like she does when things get too tough,
when she's had enough.

  Let me in, I beg,
banging on her door.
I try the handle, shout some more,
kick some furniture, stub my toe,
swear my head off, even though
no one's

    actually

      listening.

Behind my bedroom door

I unzip the case of my violin,
tighten my bow, tighten, tighten,
unwrap the rosin
glistening in its tin
like sticky amber.

I take this jewel, begin
polishing the thin
bow hairs, tuck my violin
under my chin.
It fits like a limb.

My bow strokes the strings,
a cloud of rosin dust rising,
the hairs on my skin
and all the heaviness within
lifting.

Leave her be

Best to leave her be,
Dad says wearily
when he comes in from work.
      He's covered in dust
      and it makes him look old.
We must just let it pass.
They're always coming and passing,
Mum's moods.

You mean going, I say.
Coming and going –
though I know now's not the time
to correct his English.

Dad frowns, pouts, then tuts.
Coming and passing, going, whatever!
He bats the air with his hand,
swatting the foreign words like flies.
I told you, Azadeh, it's probably hormones,
mid-life change, no big thing.
Just get on with homework, I do dinner.

He puts away his tools
and spools of wire, wound thick
like liquorice, and I suddenly wish
that I could hug him, or he me,
but Dad doesn't really
do that kind of thing,
not unless I'm crying
or bleeding, on the outside.

My reply

Phoebe's text is literally
a little light in the dark,
flashing on my pillow.
I want to tell her everything
but I decide to save it for tomorrow
when I can see her bright eyes
and her boyish voice telling me,
Look, it's probably nothing, Azzy.
Everything's going to be OK.

So I just say

PHEEEEEEEBS!
Insanely excited too
SO much to tell you . . .
smiley, heart times two
kisskisskisskisskiss

Darlington College

The cost of my school fees
would be more than Dad's whole salary
but I get to go for free,
get to wear a fancy
uniform and pretend to be
someone else.

I always get the bus.
I say it's because I don't want a fuss,
don't want to make Dad late
but it's really because I hate
his battered van with ELECTRICIAN
on the side
while everyone else
is in their big, wide
Jeeps and sleek Mercedes.

On the relief of going back to school

The gates, the quads, the windows and lawns,
the pillars, the towers, the arches that yawn.
The good morning, sir! The good morning, miss!
The predictability of all this.

The houses, the studies, assembly, roll call,
the prefects, the merits, the detentions, Hall.
The learn your lessons! The class dismissed!
The predictability of all this.

Reunion

I clamber up the many steps to Woolf House,
violin on my back, tortoise-like,
and tap in the new door code: 1882.
Our housemistress, Mrs Swift,
has stuck a sign on the door saying
    WELCOME BACK, GIRLS!
underlined with pink highlighter swirls.

Phoebe's already in the corridor
in the doorway of our Lower Sixth study
chatting to the new Fourth-formers
and a gaggle of Lower Fifths
who are lifting her new blonde braids
and admiring her tan.

Sorry to interrupt the Phoebe Fan Club,
I say. She turns around and squeals,
then we hug, rocking side to side.
It's been more than a month.
Love the hair!
   Yeah? Not too white-girl-cringe?
No, it's cool! Though I miss your fringe.
   I missed YOU!
Serves you right for going to Peru!
   Serves you right for being such a music geek.
   I told you, you could've come with
   even just for a week.
I know, I know.
I know I could never have afforded the flight.
SO, what was it like?

God, AMAZING! I mean, Machu Picchu.
Hellooooo?!
Mum actually cried, she found it sooo
'incredibly moving'.

Pheebs does her mum's silky, Radio 4 voice
perfectly, then rolls her eyes and smiles.

        Dad wants to buy a house in Peru now.
Wow, really?
        Actually I think he already has.
        You see my Instagram pics?

Of course I did
but I don't mind seeing them again.

Go on. Make me jealous then

and she does.

Peru

hashtag sungate hashtag sacredvalley
hashtag incatrail hashtag devilsbalcony
hashtag highpriesthouse hashtag royaltomb
hashtag hotsprings hashtag templeofmoon
hashtag brothers hashtag cowboys hashtag horsebacktour
hashtag headintheclouds hashtag nofilter hashtag phwoar

temple of moon

Anyway, enough about Peru, Phoebe says.
What did YOU get up to?!

I want to tell Phoebe . . .

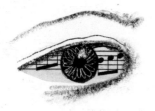

how I came home from my summer orchestra trip
to find Mum sick, but in her *mind* sick,
sobbing at the sink
till her eyes disappeared to glassy chinks,
buried in puffy pockets of wrinkled skin,
and her hair beginning to thin.

I want to tell her
how the pores on Mum's face widened
and her skin waxed and whitened,
how her cheeks went hollow
like something would swallow
her up, any minute, from the inside.

But I don't

Because Alicia's there. *Surprise!*
I'm your new study buddy!
      This wasn't what we'd planned.
      Our study was me, Pheebs, El, Tamsin, Lottie.
Disappointment rises in my throat like vomit.
I swallow it back down, feel it
churning and burning in my stomach.

Cool, hey?! Alicia says breezily.
I swapped with Lottie
because she wanted to be with Fi
and I wanted to be with Phoebe-dweebs.
      Really wish she'd stop calling her that.
Oh and you too, Az, obvs.
She shoots me a wry smile, blows an air kiss.
Oops. Sorry, missed!
Does she realise she's being a bitch?

I can never tell with Alicia.

Heading to lessons

After registration I walk ahead,
 melting into the crowd gathering round Tamsin,
who's talking at a hundred miles an hour,
her hands swinging wildly, this way and that
like some modern dance duo, interpreting
the saga of her Drama Camp romances.
I laugh in the right places but I'm only half
listening, just enjoying the bubbling sound of her voice.
It's the backing track to school beginning again,
    to my life beginning again.
Pheebs catches up, hooks onto my arm.
Bet you really missed this, she whispers,
then she does Tamsin's *drama face* uncannily well
so we swell with laughter
till it snorts out our mouths and noses
like champagne bubbles.
    Uh-oh, trouble.
    Something's set them off, Lottie scoffs
for we are known for this helpless giggling,
gasping for air, drowning
 in our own
    hilarity.

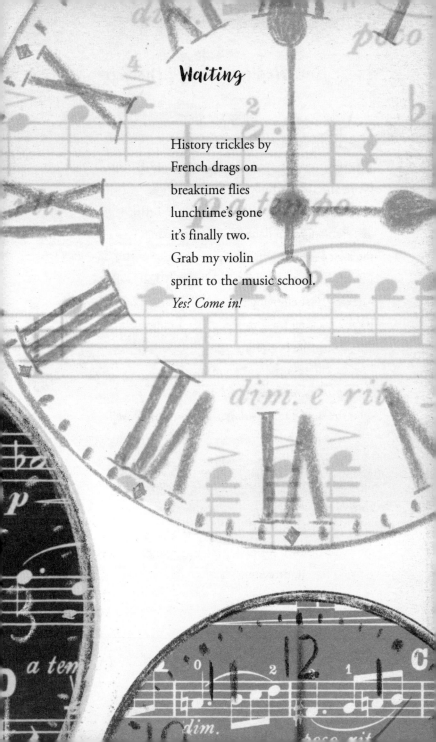

Waiting

History trickles by
French drags on
breaktime flies
lunchtime's gone
it's finally two.
Grab my violin
sprint to the music school.
Yes? Come in!

First violin lesson of the year

Margaret   playing
   doesn't   I'm   scales
     beat   whoosh!   in
       about   then   three
         the   was   octaves
           bush   summer   minor
             she how   melodic
               asks   harmonic

        until   fingers!
     tune   your   your
       in   violin's   in
       perfectly   singing   ringing
       they're   them   are
        until   back   they
        again   to   until
    Start   you

Facts I know about Margaret

She's been teaching violin for thirty years.
    She wears a chain with a tiny gold cross.
She used to have a solo career.
    Instead of *Oh God* she says *Oh gosh!*

She dyes her hair red, like autumn leaves.
    She's full-blown operatic when she sings.
She drinks weird, pungent herbal teas.
    She doesn't wear a wedding ring.

23

Party

At breaktime everyone in our study
heads to the Pret down the road
as the cafe in school is no longer cool,
according to Alicia. *We need to start drinking*
proper coffee, none of that filtered shit.
Phoebe buys mine on her card.
I try to push her my last fiver
but she waves me away.
Another day, she says.
It's always another day.
I do intend to pay her back
but admittedly I've lost track
of how much I owe her.

OK, girls, Phoebe says,
sipping her latte, *let's talk BIRTHDAYS*
The 'rents are going away
so I'm thinking . . . POOL PARTY!
Everyone shrieks, *OMGGGGGG!!*
Alicia starts dancing. *Bring. It. On.*
Even better, let's have a joint one!
Let's do it! Phoebe grins.
Let's dooo iiiit! Alicia sings
then she hugs Phoebe really tight
and I think I might
just vom.

Going home

I get off at my stop and walk to the top
of the avenue where the houses shrink
from mansions to tiny terraces
like ours, where ironically
all the streets are named
after grand composers,
Handel Road
Elgar Avenue
Britten Lane
then our street,
Purcell Way.

I like to think
they all live here,
our ghostly
neighbours,
their spirits
in the bricks,
their hearts
in the tarmac,
their musical souls
in the paving stones.

Drying up

I'm relieved to see that Mum is up and dressed,
even if she is electric with stress
like yesterday when we had our fight.
She's poring over bills tonight,
her face all scrumpled up
because Dad's work is drying up.
These days, his phone hardly rings
and if it does the customers are haggling.
Some people! he moans every day.
They think I'm working in bazaar, eh?!

Mum takes out her computer, searches for jobs again,
except this time, she's clicking on all of them:

Digital Analyst, Deputy Head
Web Developer, Head Chef

I can do anything if I just put my mind to it!
She looks up defiantly, as if
she's expecting me to strike back.
Of course, Mum. You could do anything you like.

I look at Dad and he's pretending he hasn't heard,
rearranging his tool cupboard for the third
time this week.
I wish he'd just speak,
rearrange some words in his head
instead.

My dream

I often dream about being a really famous violinist
like Yehudi Menuhin or Jascha Heifetz.
Then I could make us all rich
so Dad wouldn't have to fix
another plug or socket
ever again in his life, no more electrics,
and Mum wouldn't worry herself sick
about paying bills, about any of it.

If that doesn't work out, I'll be a poet
because words pop into my head like music,
pulsing, beating, pumping quick
like the way fingers click or seconds tick,
only poetry won't make you rich
which is pretty unfair
considering all the people on YouTube blaring
        utter shit
and getting paid *heaps* for it.

Next morning

My toast burns
because Dad's turned up
the knob on the toaster again,
which then sets off the smoke alarm,
which he fitted too close to the kitchen
and now it's **screaming**

the

house

down,

and there was me,
trying to be
as quiet as a mouse
so Mum can have a lie-in.

Dad does the drill, runs
like the room is on fire, slams
the kitchen door behind him, BAM!
Fans, fans the alarm like a madman
until the stupid thing's placated.

He slots two new slices of bread
into the toaster. *Sit down.*
I make you more.

>   *No, I'm going to be late, Dad.*
>   *My bus leaves in eight minutes.*

No, Azadeh, I take you to school today.

>   Oh, great.

Lift

The letters on his van are chipped
and he still hasn't fixed
that big dent.
The inside smells of air freshener, minty trees
and a hint of cigarettes underneath.

He's stopped smoking in front of me
though I know that he's still hooked.
Dad puts on the radio, probably so
we don't have to talk,
tapping his fingers on the wheel
to some nineties pop song, beating like a drummer.
It's not bad in fact, actually
kinda catchy, but the chorus begins
to get under my skin so I suddenly
change the station to Classic FM
without asking him.

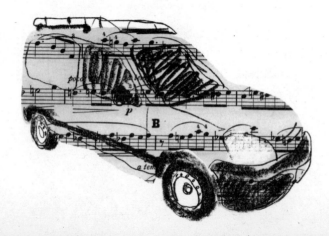

Dad just tuts under his breath
     arguing is like death to him
and to top it off, it's one of those
loud, modern pieces that make no sense
so it's making him all tense.

As we approach my school, I remind him
to drop me off a bit before, on the corner.
Here's fine, I say, tugging at the door.
He slows obediently and I tumble out
like I'm in an action movie, mumbling
     Bye, you can go now, thanks,
and I see him watching those big black tanks
gliding
          ahead
                    through
                              the school gates
and I wonder
     if he hates them
as much as
     I hate his van.

Licence

Jamie Weir in the year above
pulls up in the quad
in his new electric-blue Mini Cooper
topped with a Union Jack.
We know that he was the first to drive
because we've all been eyeing
the Upper Sixth's independence
with jealousy.
Feels like forever until we
can do the same. In the study, we're already
talking of road trips round Europe together.
They reckon I'll pass my test first time
and Tamsin will blag her way through
so we'll do most of the driving.
As for Phoebe and El, well they'll probably
fail a few times on account of their zero
spatial awareness/dreamy-distracted selves
so they'll be the ones who'll blast out tunes
and stick their heads out the sunroof
WOOOHOOOOOOOOOOOOO!

Pub

Dad's not home for dinner again.
Mum says that he's 'working late',
trying her best to hide her strain
as the food goes cold upon his plate.

Learning the violin

I started when
I was seven.
My primary school
gave us one or two
music lessons, lent
us different instruments.
My favourite was the violin,
       the way it looked, even,
        with the curves of a person
then we found Margaret's number fluttering
on a bulletin board at the library.
She was expensive but Mum insisted.

At first I sounded a bit
like a cat being strangled
or me when my hair was tangled
and Mum had to comb out the tats.
I'd scrape the strings, back
and forth, back and forth
like I had a saw
instead of a bow
and I was so slow
at learning the notes
that I wanted to throw
the violin against the wall
then crunch all
the pieces
like I was eating
broken biscuits.
Yeah, weird, I know.

Margaret taught me patience though,
the real meaning of time,
and soon my fingers could easily slide,
my bow glide,
dip and dive
until my violin was singing
to me, deeply like it was tunnelling
my soul, high
like it had swallowed the sky.

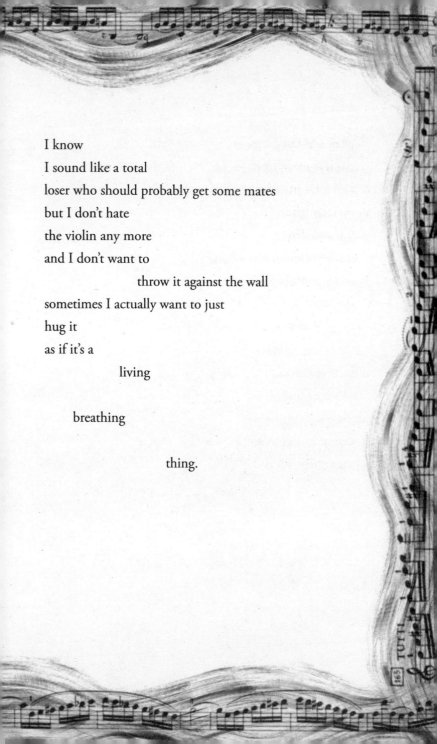

I know
I sound like a total
loser who should probably get some mates
but I don't hate
the violin any more
and I don't want to

throw it against the wall

sometimes I actually want to just
hug it
as if it's a

living

breathing

thing.

English class

English with Miss Keats
is better than any other subject – it beats
A level Music even.
I'm always last
to leave her class.
I wish it could go on and on,
even if she does go off on a tangent
quite a bit
    literary meandering, she calls it
but it is interesting
if that's your thing.
She likes calling
me to read, says I have
a musical way of speaking,
whatever that means.

School orchestra practice

It's my second year as leader of school orchestra
even though you're not supposed to do it twice, as a rule
but there was no one else to choose from,
except maybe Rupert Singer-Kingsmith
in Upper Sixth, who sits next to me
and plays his violin as if it's a cheese grater.

This term Mr T. let me choose the piece
    'Mars' from Holst's *Planets* suite.
When the violins realise they get to play
with the wooden bits of their bows,
their minds are blown. *Nooooo waaaay!*
they say, whacking the strings.
It has to be GEN-TLE! Mr T. sings.
Azadeh will demonstrate.

I turn my bow upside down
and let it bounce out the quaver triplets.
The trick is keeping your arm light,
getting the weight and fall just right.

Wonderful! Mr T. whispers. *You see,*
it's simply a distant drumbeat,
like the pulse of the galaxy.
Dadada
> *da,*
>> *da,*
>>> *dada da.*
Dadada
> *da,*
>> *da,*
>>> *dada da.*

The Governors'
Autumn Reception

Mr T. reminds me, *Don't forget, this evening you're expected*
at the headmaster's house for that dreadful reception.
Play the usual Kreisler–Schubert–Bach background mix
while the governors mingle with their drinks.
Then they'll probably want to chat to you for a bit,
so look interesting!

                                                 Yes, sir. I'll try, I lie.

Interesting

Where is your unusual name from?
And do you know what it means?
So, do you speak Farsi then?
Oh, you haven't ever been?!

Did your father flee the revolution?
Is that why he never went back?
Do you still have family over there?
Are the women as oppressed as all that?

So what brings you to Darlington?
Oh, aren't these scholarships good?
We waived a Syrian's fees, you know?
That'd be thirty thousand, that would!

Netball

We slip on our bright bibs and Mrs Giggs splits
us up into two teams, clearly As and Bs
though we're really more like Ds,
except for Phoebe who's actually a pretty
good wing attack, when she concentrates.

Alicia's the A-team's trusty goal shooter.
  She looks even bustier in her bib,
thrusting chest passes between her and Lottie,
who's goal attack. Finally she catches the ball,
grips it between her glittery fingernails.

  Man her, Azzyyyy! Tamsin shrieks
  because she takes her captaining of the Bs (Ds)
                                    very seriously
  and also because I'm goal defence,
  supposedly on account of my long arms. Don't ask.

I stretch them out far in front of me,
my hands hovering frantically over the ball,
up and down and left and right,
wherever Alicia moves it,
as if she's clasping a magnetic jewel
that's controlling my every movement.

Suddenly, with a bend and flick

she sends it s p i n i n g through the air.

I already know I'll leap too late, and I turn midway
to see it, tumbling round the rim of the goal
before it's swallowed whole
by the scraggy throat
of the net.

Don't look so glum, girls, Alicia says with a grin.
You haven't lost . . . YET.

After school

Some Fridays, I get the school minibus back to Pheebs's.
We tell our parents we're doing our French essays
but it's just an excuse to make playlists
of all the music we're currently obsessed with.

God I'm glad you're here, Pheebs sighs
when one of the boys lets off yet another fart
(it's either that or chat about boobs or barfs).
Hate being the only girl on this bus.

We have code names for them all, which helps.
There's *Fitty McPsycho, Nuclear Stinkbomb,*
Pervy Paul Starton's *Porn Stardom*, and so on.
It makes the journey go that little bit quicker.

When they finally get off at their stops,
we rate their houses on a scale of twattishness.
Sports cars and tacky statues are best.
That gets them triple points.

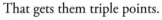

Phoebe's house

I've missed this glinting hallway
with its twisting chandelier, sparkling marble,
its walls crowded with silver-framed family photos,
like shiny trophies.
I slip off my shoes in the boot room, choose
one of the many pairs of slippers left for guests
then pass into the living room, where sunlight pours
majestically through the yawning windows.

Hi, girls! Phoebe's mum chimes from the kitchen.
How lovely to see you, Azadeh!
    Hi, Mrs Baxter, you too. She hugs us both,
clinging on to Phoebe a little longer,
rubbing her back. *How was your day, darling?*

Fine, Phoebe sighs. *Too much homework though.*

    I should think so, her mum replies,

    downing the rest of her wine.

    That's what we're paying for, after all!

Phoebe turns and rolls her eyes so only I can see.

    Do help yourself to refreshments, girls.

    Marisa's put fresh OJ in the fridge.

Please don't call it OJ, Mum, it really doesn't suit you.

She replies with something about being down with the kids,

which makes Phoebe cringe and signal our escape

so we pad away up the stairs, which are snug

with honey-cream carpets, still as clean

as if they'd been fitted that very morning.

Playlist

We open Phoebe's window and climb out
        onto the roof terrace
            like we always do,
                even though we're not supposed to.
Phoebe brings her speaker and we scroll through
new R&B releases on her phone, adding them to
    Our Latest Playlist,
which is already full of Janelle Del Rey,
our fave, the lady of rhythm and bass,
with her husky, honey-thick voice
slipping seamlessly between melody
and quick-tongued rap
which we rat-a-tat-tat through our teeth,
delightfully, devotedly
like we're chanting hymns.

Phoebe's parents

The dark begins to set in outside.
Stay for supper, they say,
we'll book you a ride.

   But my bus, my bus, my bus.

Sleep over then, Phoebe pleads.
It'll be so much fun,
just what we need.

   But I can't, I can't, I can't.

My mum's cooked dinner already,
she sent me a text,
they're waiting, it's ready.

   Another time, another time, another time.

And I run, back into the night
while they wave at me
warm, in the light

   out of sight, out of sight, out of sight.

White lie

Dinner's not already ready
Mum's not waiting for me.
The text's actually
from Dad.

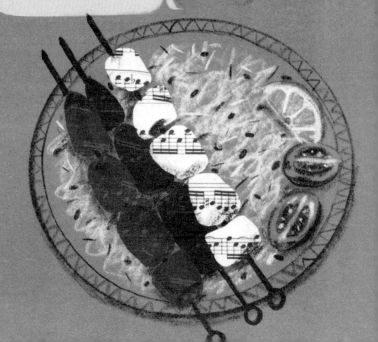

When you back?
Mum having kip
you want fish & chips
or shall I grab
Persian kebab?
Dad xx

Kebab

We go out in the end, leaving Mum to rest.
She says she already ate, though we know
    it's probably not true.
Dad drives us to Norouz and we sit in the window
on the rickety chairs, listening to the sizzling grill.
We came here together when Mum was last ill,
except that time it passed in days
and now it's been weeks.
I open my mouth to speak
but Dad's frowning at his phone
then the owner, Ozhan, comes over
and our window for conversation closes.
    Salām, Ali-jān, kam peydāyid!
Salām, Ozhan, che khoobe ke shomā ro bāz mibinam,
Dad replies, smiling in a way that only his language can make
him do.
    Hāl-e shomā chetore? Ozhan asks.
Dad nods. *Khoobam, mersi, khodā rā shokr.*
I've never learned Farsi but I recognise these long greetings,
the how are you's, the polite non-truths, all the God-be-willings.
Ozhan looks at me and says something I don't understand.
I look blankly at Dad and he searches for words.
He's always so slow to translate and it grates on my nerves.

He's, er, saying –

>*I say you have beautiful eyes, chesm-ha*, Ozhan explains.

>*Like my daughter's. Ghashang. Beautiful.*

Like so many times when I hear my father's tongue,

I open my mouth to reply

as if Farsi is a song I know so well in my head

but cannot sing,

like I'm missing

different vocal cords

a different mouth

different heart

different skin.

Oh. Thank you, I say

in my clunky, less melodious mother tongue.

>*You not speak Farsi then?*

I shake my head. Ozhan tuts at Dad,

reprimands him with questions that don't have answers.

Dad defends himself with shrugs and hand gestures.

>*My Azadeh-jān speak English like the Queen.*

>*It's all she needs.*

55

All she needs is

All she needs is
a visa to her father's homeland
to feel the heat on her skin of the scorching sun
under which he was born.

All she needs is
true answers to the *Why did you really leave?*
Do you still grieve for your parents? For your country?
Or is it for everything you hoped to achieve?

All she needs is
to see her cousins in the flesh,
compare the bumps in their noses, the weight
of the lids of their eyes and their shy, skinny limbs.

All she needs is
to not just hear about the perfume
of almond trees, pomegranates and goje sabz plums
but to smell them for herself and make her own memories.

All she needs is
for all these words not to be foreign,
for them to be hers and his and ours so that nothing
feels secret between them, nothing's unspoken any more.

Breaking bread

The skewers of freshly grilled meat hiss and spit
on our plates, forming bridges over bright saffron rice.
Ozhan brings us tomato and okra stew, *khoresht bamieh*,
cold cucumber yoghurt, *mast-o-khiar*, and my favourite,
the flatbread, *sangak*, which I rip and dip into the sauces.

Why didn't you teach me Farsi? I ask Dad, suddenly,
before I even know I wanted to.
Why do I only know Persian words if it's on a menu?
> *Well, you know those, at least.*
> *You know what you eat,* Dad smirks.
But I'm in no mood to joke.
I hoped you'd give me a better answer than needing to speak
the Queen's bloody English.
> *Please, do not swear, Azadeh.*
That's not swearing, Dad.
He looks up from his food and stops chewing, supposedly
a sign for me to retreat, which I don't.

Maybe you can teach me some swear words in Farsi, hey?
Ahmagh! Goh! Pedarsukteh!

> *Azadeh*, Dad warns,

not daring to turn his head to see if Ozhan is looking.
What?! I've heard YOU use them.

> *Why you being like this?*

Like WHAT?

> *You don't think I got enough to worry about*
> *without stupid thing like this?*
> *Deh, just finish your food!*

He tuts and goes back to his meal, which he eats in misery
while I watch, half ashamed, half pleased,
because at least now he looks exactly how I feel.

Have you seen?

Mum's been watching the news on a loop.
Turn it off, it's not good for you, Dad tuts.
You been watching this immigrant stuff all day.

> *This stuff? This STUFF?*
> *This STUFF is people's lives, Ali!*
> *We can't just turn a blind eye!*

Mum looks back at the TV screen,
the images flickering over her face,
making her skin distraught,
her eyes even more haunted.

> *If we all just thought about others before*
> *ourselves, we wouldn't be in this mess.*
> *We have to DO something!*
> *We have to do something NOW*
> *before it's all too late!*

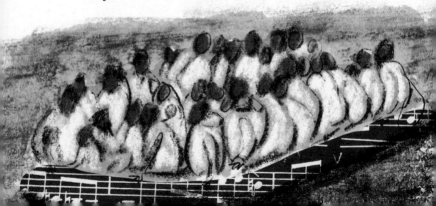

Dad shakes his head and walks away
like he's afraid to say
anything that might
                    tip Mum over the edge.

He goes and sits at his little desk
in the back room,
not even pretending to do
anything,
            just sitting
                        and staring.

My stomach flares
with dread, my feet
curl into the carpet
                like the
                            gnarled roots
            of a strange tree,
                        making me
                unable
                        to

                                move.

Orchestra practice

Mr T. says he has some exciting news,
which we know is never going to be exciting, except –

    Here he is! he cries. *Our new addition to Planet Mars.*

    Welcome, earthling!

I turn to see Jamie Weir, cradling
a bass drum in his arms.

    Ladies and gentlemen, our charming percussionist!

Errrrr, I just play the drums, sir. Jamie smiles dubiously.

    I'm afraid you'll be playing a gong and cymbals too,

                                      says Mr. T.,

    and hopefully the timpani, if the bloody

    bursar eventually increases our music budget!

English

The lads are giving Miss Keats
the usual backchat
when she slams an extract
down on each of our desks,
from a book called *Shakespeare,*
The Invention of the Human
by Harold Bloom.
Loudmouth Louis O'Toole
says, *Miss, what's this got to do*
with our A level exam?
It's way too hard!
Miss Keats folds her arms
and tells us her dad
had recommended it.
Is he a professor, miss?
Is he the examiner, miss?
Louis, under his breath,
No, he's just a dick!

Then Miss Keats says,
very matter-of-factly,
Actually, he's a builder
who loves literature
and the lads nearly lose it then,
pissing themselves laughing,
squirming in their seats,
not even trying
to hide their hilarity,
though I can't even see
what is so funny.

Miss Keats keeps her dignity,
completely ignores them
and makes Louis read.
He snorts his way
through the first sentences,
where he basically says
Shakespeare was the most important
writer ever
in the history of the world.

Later, I Tipp-ex his words
onto the inside
of my English file,
in funky lettering.
I'm not sure why.
Maybe because the words
sound impressive
or maybe because I want
Miss Keats to know
I'm on her side.

Harold
Bloom

Presents

We're hanging in the study when Alicia asks Phoebe,
Whaddya want for your birthday, bitch?
Then gives Pheebs an interminable list
of Things I'd Never Be Able To Afford.

Do you wanna Tiffany bracelet? A Polaroid printing machine?
That T-shirt by Alexander McQueen?
How about a facial toning device? A Burberry cashmere hat?
Gold hoops? This (gross) *Gucci baseball cap?*

Oh crap.

So what do I get her?

P hoebe gives the best gifts, always impeccably wrapped

R ibbon hugging some thick, glittery paper tight, hiding

E stée Lauder perfume, a Lancôme Juicy Tube, Diesel jeans for
my sixteenth.

S o what do I get her? The girl who can buy anything.

E arrings, earphones, eyeshadow?

N ope.

T ickets to see Janelle Del Rey? YES!

S hit. That's a hundred quid at best!

Busking

Whenever I need money, I busk for it
especially at Christmas when I can make a hundred quid,
one fifty if I go to the posher end of town.
Today I go to our local high street
so I know I won't bump into anyone from school
just lots of generous OAPs who probably
feel a bit sorry for me. They say things like

> *Oh, isn't that lovely, dear!*
> *Your parents must be proud.*
> *You do have parents, don't you? Just checking!*
> *You never know, with all these immigrants!*
> *You do look a bit Syrian, you know!*

Sometimes I get requests.
Can you do that one from Schindler's List?
Give us a bit of Four Seasons!
By the end of the day I've got fifty-six quid in change,
    enough for one concert ticket,
and a five-pound note from a woman
who asked me to play 'The Swan' again,
then cried.

The Swan

I first heard it
on the radio
when Mum was listening
to Classic FM
over breakfast.
I was maybe
nine or ten.
I stopped eating
my Coco Pops
and my eyes
began to sting,   I remember
my heartbeat   my arms tingling and looking
quickened,   down at the hairs as if feathers
it felt as if   might be growing there. Over the rippling piano
the melody   notes, the cello glided mournfully and I
was draping   couldn't decide whether I was devastated or deeply
itself onto   happy, or both. In any case, it was the most
my skin.   beautiful thing my recently pierced ears had ever heard.

Mum's homework

What are you doing? Mum asks, as she pushes my door ajar.
> *Homework*, I answer, without looking up.
I can see that. Which subject?
> *English.*
You still got that young one? Miss —
> *Keats, yup.*
She was nice. Very clever. You always liked her.
> *Mmm.*
Went to Oxford, didn't she? Or was it Cambridge?
> *Oxford.*

I'm doing my own homework, you know.
I don't actually want to know. I dread to think
what crazy idea has gripped her now
but I sense she's going to tell me anyway.
*I'm doing something about all those poor refugees,
Azadeh. I'm going to save them.*

I bite my tongue because the tone of her voice
is so alien, it's making me angry.
Anything could fly out of my mouth right now.

I'm going to buy a big house to put them all in.
I found a place in town that's perfect.
I think the bank will agree, you know?
I spoke to someone today, they were extremely positive,
said it was a very worthy project.
I've just got to fill in all this paperwork now –
         wish me luck!

She shuts the door
                    rushes off downstairs
leaving all that shit   suspended in the air.

Wish me luck, more like!

The argument

It's rare that Mum and Dad shout it out.
Their rows are usually low-key affairs
quickly swept under the rug,
     and there are plenty of them in our house,
     beautiful, Persian ones,
     mazed with complex patterns
but tonight Dad's cracked too
he's blown a fuse
can't do this any longer
can't keep on being the stronger
one and he calls her a word
he can't take back.
    You a maniac
and that is that.
Mum packs a bag,
takes the keys, starts the car
and the engine growls
with the threat of her departure
to God
       Knows
           Where.

Wait!

I run out into the street with no shoes on,
hoping the neighbours don't witness this scene,
      but Eileen's curtains
                  are already twitching.

      I bang on the windscreen.
          Please wait for me.
          You can't go alone, I'll keep you company!
Of course I really mean
          I'll stop you from crashing the car
          and killing people, including yourself!

She rolls the window down,
cuts the engine and tells me

                        Five minutes
                        else I'm leaving.

She's clearly serious.   My heart heaves.

Why doesn't she need me

          like I need her?

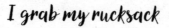

I grab my rucksack

But how do you pack
when you don't know where you're going
or when you're coming back
or if you're coming back at all?
Part of me hopes that
we won't come back, that we can have
a miraculous fresh start or some such crap
and that maybe all this was because
Mum's just unhappy with Dad,
it's all just been cracks in their marriage,
not Mum that's

                cracked.

Not OK

Dad is in the garden with his back turned,
hunched against the freezing wind and drizzle,
sucking on a cigarette as if it's his last.
Dad, I'm going with Mum.
  OK, he says, glancing over his shoulder
so I don't see him smoking.
OK? Is that all he can say?!
I want to shake him by the shoulders, shout in his face,
Mum is leaving you! Wake up, why don't you?!
But I hear the engine turn back on

                              so I run.

Dad the ostrich

It doesn't bury its head in the sand.
This is what's called a popular myth,
like lemmings jumping off cliffs
or crocodiles being slow on land.

The ostrich runs from danger, fast,
wings outstretched like an aeroplane,
like a child playing a game
and hoping to take off at last.

The reason you can't see its head
is, when the danger's close at hand
it lies down, flattens its neck on the sand
and pretends that it's already dead.

Downpour

Mum speeds   through dark   lashing   rain   and the wipers

are going   crazy   like they   can't keep up   like any

minute   they'll fly right off   I ask her   where we're going

what exactly   did Dad say   why is she running away   and now

she's muttering   her words   pitter-pattering   Maniac   I'll

give him maniac   just because   I was   sick   with you

that was   sixteen years ago   how dare he   dig that up

why is he   digging all that   up again?   Bloody

men   Mum   what do you mean?   Suddenly

her jaw   clenches shut   she grips   the steering wheel   tight

then drives   drives   drives   through the   blinding   lights.

Text from Phoebe

Hey bae, you ok?
you still coming out tonight?
meeting on beach by Bar Latina
hasta luego, bambina!
kisskisskisskisskiss

Hard shoulder

We stop on the hard shoulder of the M25.
Mum needs to close her eyes
just for five minutes
cos she hasn't slept
in three whole days,
     which she suddenly reveals
     like it's no big deal
then she puts her head on the wheel
like she's crashing in slow motion.

The cars and lorries are whizzing past.
My heart is racing fast. No one can see us.
     I switch the warning lights on.
Isn't it dangerous stopping here? I ask Mum.
In the dark, on the hard shoulder?

As I say it, I imagine we're sitting on the actual hard shoulder
of a concrete giant, like that book
we did in primary school, *The Iron Man*
then suddenly, we are
              falling
                    falling
                         down.

Headphones

I cannot sleep but I
can block out all this noise,
put two shells over my ears,
hear the roar
of a symphonic sea,
a concerto of falling leaves,
a starry nocturne,
a kaleidoscopic rhapsody,
and pretend to be
in another world.

Waiting for God

When she wakes up, Mum is dead still,
as if she hasn't really woken up at all.

Can we go now? I whisper
like I'm quietly defusing a bomb.

I'm waiting, she says,
still looking away.

For what?
For a sign.

From who?
From God.

And then I know
we're screwed.

Maybe it's me

From the day you are born you want to believe
that every word your mother says is true,
        don't you?

Otherwise, what are you going to do?
Who are you going to believe, if not your mum?
                That's right, no one.

So you'll believe her at any cost
even when it's clear she's lost

                                her mind.

In fact, you'd rather believe
that you're the one who's gone and lost
        yours.

It's definitely better than believing your mum
is no longer The One
                you can trust.

Talking her down

Mum wants to keep on driving
though she won't tell me where we're driving to.
Don't you tell me what I can and cannot do,
she says in a tone I don't recognise
but despise.

I just think it's best we stop to rest,
I say. *You always tell me everything's better*
in the morning. The roads are dangerous in the rain
and this traffic's a pain.
We can set off first thing.
Let's get off at the next exit, grab a drink.
OK?
I'll find us a B&B, like we're on holiday!
Besides, I'm starving, we really should eat.

Eat, of course, she says, shaking her head,
then she looks at me like she's suddenly remembered
I'm her daughter and she's my mum
                                        and we do need to eat.

Next exit

It's only six
more miles
but it feels like
six thousand.
Mum crawls along,
hands trembling
on the wheel.
Better too slow
than too fast,
I guess,
but behind us
cars are
beeping
swerving
cursing
and now
is the time
I wish I knew
how
    the hell
        to drive.

Car park

It's not exactly a B&B
but Mum is suddenly
exhausted again
    and winds back her seat
                till it's as flat as it can go.
Why don't we just sleep here for the night? she says
but it's not really a question.
She rests her hands on her lap
and I want to believe that
this is some British Airways ad
and she's in a reclining first-class seat
going somewhere really cool and fast
and someone's going to bring her an eye mask
any minute and a glass of champagne
but in reality, we're in a place called Staines
in some dodgy car park
sitting deep in the dark
of our battered Ford Escort.

Another text from Phoebe

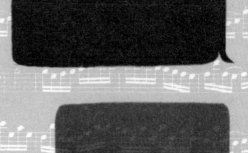

Helloooooo?

Azzyyyyyyyyy?

Night burger

While Mum's capsized into sleep
I creep out of the car
and walk down the dimly lit street
looking for something, anything, to eat
but everything's shut, windows shadowy
with the ghosts of chairs.

Then suddenly it's there,
on the corner: *McDonald's!*
Golden and promising!
Phoebe made me hate it ever since she showed me
pictures of half-electrocuted cows, but now
I'm starving and there's nowhere else to go
so I order an XL Big Mac meal, with extra nuggets
for Mum, in case she wakes up.

I sink my teeth into
the sweet, fake-tasting meat,
wolf down handfuls of chips,
slathered in sauce,
pour Coke down my throat
to wash it all down
until there's only tinkling ice left,
slinking to the bottom of the cup.

When I'm done,
I crush all the boxes into one,
slip the debris into the bin
then go to the bathroom.
There, I wash the day
off my face, comb
its knots out of my hair, brush
its bits from my teeth,
because even though
we're going to sleep in the car,
I still need my routine, need to feel
there's still some normality left
in all this mess.

Falling asleep

I fall
but not into sleep
I fall
deep into the freezing night
I fall
deep down into a dark where anything might
haul
me away, where anything might
crawl
into Mum's brain and take her from me once and
for all

a scrawl
of smoky clouds swirl into the outline of ghosts,
they call
to me, warn me that *someone is breaking into the car*,
footfalls,
the sound of this dark is the thump of unknown doors and
the *wrawl*
of far-off cats, possibly foxes, despairing in unison at the moon,
and the squall
of sirens surging across the city

                                        to someone in danger.

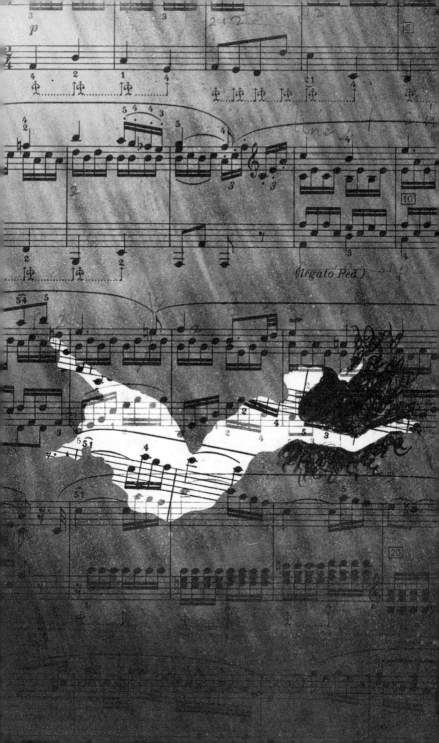

Dream

When I finally, briefly sleep
    I dream of spiral staircases
        like the one leading up to the room
            where I took my Grade 8 violin exam,
                except this time Mum isn't behind me
                    telling me my stomach ache will pass –
                Drink some water, take those herbal drops I got you!
        Instead she's ahead of me, already in the room,
      and the examiner is examining her in my place
except she's holding the violin all wrong,
      bow in her left hand, strings under her right
          and she's gripping everything so tight
                there's no way she can play a single note
                    let alone that Mendelssohn Allegro!
        I try to run into the room and tell them to stop,
      that there's been some kind of mix-up,
    but a woman blocks my way.
No children here, I hear her say.
    I look at Mum for help and she winks at me
      like she might have a plan, but before I can ask,
        before I can say, 'Please don't drop my violin!'
          the door has already slammed in my face.

Morning

When the darkness lifts the dawn light sifts
down on me
like flour
falling
softly
into a bowl,
predictably,
satisfyingly,
mixing with
familiar
ingredients:
the first whoosh
of cars, sharp
birdsong,
the tumble
of rubbish bins,
the rumble
of shop shutters

until the promise of day is
baking in the oven and
rising, like Mum's
sponge cake.

Awake

I'm about to
reply to Phoebe's texts
when Mum wakes up
and I remember that this day
will be no piece of cake.
She stares at the grey car ceiling
then bolts upright, gasping for air, like she's
been held underwater.

Can we go home, Mum?
I say quietly, quickly, desperately.
I really think we should.
She looks out of the windows, checks the mirrors
then turns her face to me, suddenly
small, squirrel-like, eyes wide with panic.
But I can't drive! she whispers.
How did I get here?
Was it
you?

The M-word

If I tell,
what will people think?

Your mum's got a screw loose
unhinged
unglued
cracked
crazed

she's a basket case
a lunatic
moonstruck
off her rocker

she's cuckoo
fell out of her tree
got bats in the belfry
and rats in the attic

she's out of her mind
not in her right mind
not all there
away with the fairies
the lights are on but no one's at home
cos she's out to lunch
not playing with a full deck of cards
lost her marbles
nutty as a fruitcake
crackers
bananas
barmy

They'll think my mum
is
barking MAD.

Well, isn't she?

Low battery

10% of battery remaining
Low Power Mode
Close

uh

oh

Last phone call

Hello, Dad? Can you hear me?

        What about now?

Hang on, I'll get out of the car.

Can you hear me now?

        I AM staying still!

I don't have much battery left.

        I said, I don't have much battery left!

Can you just come and get us, please?

Mum's not . . .

        she got much worse

We're in a car park

        I don't know exactly!

I'll send you our location.

        On the Maps app!

Well, I'll text you the address then.

Just hurry, please?

        Hello? Dad?   Dad?

        Can you hear me?

        Dad?

Dad

I've never been so relieved to see Dad's van
appearing in the rear-view mirror like a long-lost relative,
bright white eyes in the morning fog,
number plate like eccentric teeth
    and the familiar shape of him
    through the windscreen
    hunched over the wheel.

He gets out and I go to him.
We hug and I feel his stubble rub against my cheek.
I close my eyes but he's   already pulling away.
How is she? he asks,   already walking away.

Mum shuffles over and Dad takes her place.
Wait! I say. *What about your van?*
Dad glances at it in the mirror.
    Oh, it can go on scrapheap.
    I get me a nice big BMW, eh?
    What you think?
He turns and winks at me
and I feel my cheeks burn up.
Don't worry about my van, Azadeh.
I take train to pick it up, another day.

Home

When we arrive, Mum goes into the living room and stares forever
at the shelves that are full of all her knick-knacks, the blue-swirl
bowls she made, floral photo frames, her Russian-doll cats.
Her hands hover over them and eventually she picks
them up but quickly puts them back, as if
they belong to somebody else.

Dinner

Dad makes us all *sabzi* rice and lets it burn on purpose,
making a layer of crunch on the bottom, called *tadig*.
It comes off in one piece, like a cake.
It's one of the few things he can make
and it does smell good, but I could murder
some of Mum's lasagne right now.

Dad opens a big can of tuna, tips a bit
onto each of our plates. *Me and Mum always make
this dish when we lived in bedsit. Remember, Kathy?*
Mum smiles weakly, picks up her fork,
but nothing more than the odd grain or flake
goes in, the rest she shuffles around her plate.
*I got your favourite dessert in fridge, you know,
Toffee sticky pudding and cream!* Dad exclaims.
Come on, Kathy, he says, waving the spoon in front of her.
Make small effort for us . . . please?

Mum's eyes well up and suddenly I have to get up.
I can't watch this excruciating scene,
Dad with his spoon and Mum like a silent baby
    who wants to scream.

César Franck Sonata for Violin and Piano in A Major

1st Movement. Allegro ben moderato

In my head I hear the piano notes
that Margaret usually plays for me,
trickling a stream four bars long
till I dive in with the melody.

I swim in it now, shoulder deep,
the vibrato bright and shimmering,
my fingers fast like quivering fish
slipping up and down the string.

I reach the high notes, *sempre dolce*,
always sweet, until it hurts
and then my soul swells up so much
I feel my body about to burst.

Back to school

Dad insists I go to school on Monday
and takes the day off work to stay with Mum
which he really can't afford to do
not at the moment
he could lose this job
and it's a good customer
a guy with a few flats in town
Dad never turns him down,
because he pays him well
and on time
It will be fine, he says
seeing my worried face
as I race out the door
in my never-ending

                    rush

                             for the bus.

Morning assembly

Good job I didn't stay at home.
It's the first Monday of the month,
     my turn to do school assembly.
It's Mrs Swift who reminds me,
You can leave registration early
Azadeh.   OK?
     OK, I say, frowning.
Mrs Swift's mouth twists sideways.
Hmm, it's not like you
to forget your musical duties.
Everything alright, Azadeh?
     Yep, fine, I say. *Just a bit sleepy, miss.*
OK, well, make sure you get some rest, after this.

As music scholars,
each one of us is collared into
playing in assembly, one every morning,
like minstrels at a medieval court.
It makes you feel important,
standing in front of the altar
bathed in stained-glass light
while the whole school looks on
and listens and applauds you
then the teachers stop you in the hallways
to tell you it was *wonderful,*
impressive, first class,
you've got a real feel for Bach!

Bach Violin Concerto in A minor

1st Movement. Allegro moderato

I'm bright-eyed,
head high, gracious,
strong, swift,
flourishing
peals of semiquavers
twisting in and out
of the piano
as if in a courtly dance,
fingers galloping,
bow gallantly
springing
from string to string,
unpacking centuries,
weaving tapestries
fit for royalty.

Facing Phoebe

Phoebe's always sweet,
so when she's salty it really stings.
Why didn't you answer any of my texts?
she says, barely bothering to look at me.
    I had stuff going on.
Do you wanna be any more vague? she huffs.
    My parents had this fight.
What, ALL weekend?
    No, but . . .
Phoebe frowns, looks like she's about to
ask something, when Alicia glides in.

Ooh, why you lookin' so SERIOUS, ladies?
Where were you on Friday night, Azzywazzy?
    She'd better not be calling me that now.
Lemme guess, you were making out with your violin?
    Alicia, Phoebe mutters.
What?! I MEAN because you were
awesome in assembly this morning.
You kill on that violin!
But you do need to get out more,
that's for sure!

Guest list

At morning break
Alicia says, *OK, party planners!*
We need to think NAMES
and she's already clicking on her phone
faster than the speed of sound.
Let's start with guys. Obviously Jay
     the twenty-something 'singer' she's seeing
and his mate, hey Pheebs?!
Whatshisname? NATE! She elbows her hard
and winks. Phoebe half laughs
then her cheeks flush red.
She looks at me all embarrassed,
like I'm her mum or something.
And you, Azadeh, Alicia says.
Who are you inviting?

Who am I inviting?

When I was on my orchestra course,
for three weeks I was stalked
by a gangly thirteen-year-old
who played bassoon and had bad BO
        so that was definitely a no.
I fancied the tall guy on double bass,
Daniel de la Mare. He had the face
of an angel or that curly-haired guy on Mum's CD,
                Jim somebody
from *The Doors*,
            but of course
I didn't speak
to him in the whole three weeks,
not once, let alone
get his phone
number.

I consider spewing a total lie
Yeah, I might invite a guy
from my orchestra
but then they'll want all the deets
and I'll seem like a total freak
if they find out it's not true
which they will do, within two
minutes of Instagramming him
and seeing he's way too fit
and that I'm in none of his pics.

Besides, Phoebe can see
right through me.

Who the hell's Nate?

At lunchtime, we go down the road to McFitties
even though I hate their shitty sandwiches
that cost six quid and sound as if
someone died in the making
e.g. quinoa-crusted crayfish and wild Moroccan rocket
on toasted 'Ezekiel' bread, whoever Ezekiel is.
We call it McFitties cos Alicia fancies the guy,
ergo he's a fitty, and the Mc is because
it's basically the McDonald's of Darlington College.

I feel Phoebe wanting to avoid me
but the pavement is narrow and inevitably
we're walking side by side, so I ask her
what I'm dying to know, maybe so
she doesn't ask me any more about Friday.
So, who the hell's Nate? Or don't you want to say?
      Oh, just some guy, a snog. Alicia was getting off
      with Jay and he was there. And you weren't.
So you would have snogged me instead then?
      Phoebe cracks a smile. *Yeah, obvs. You're hot.*
      You gonna tell me about your parents' fight or what?

Nothing

Behind us in the street
the girls stumble and shriek
while Pheebs piles up her hair on top of her head,
twists it, quickly clamps it in place.
I think of her warm house, the space
in her neat jewellery drawer where
that silver hair clip came from.
Oh, it was nothing, I say.
They're OK now.

                    What were they fighting about?
Not really sure.
Just a lot of shouting.

                    Must've been serious though.
                    You missed our freezing-ass beach party yo!
I know, I know.
I could've done with those mojitos.

                    But they're OK now, you say?
                    She pushes the door of the cafe,
                    holds it open for me.
Yeah, I say, vaguely.
They probably will be.

Texting with Dad

How's Mum?

OK
Been sleeping most of day

You took her to the GP?

No
She won't go

Why not?

Says she's got it under control
No need for meds
Says it's her head
And she's knows what's inside it

Make her go!
Or phone Dr O.

She won't let me

Oh for God's sake!
I'll do it then

Lesson with Margaret

Margaret can read me like a book
or a music score.
My dear, you're not at your best today.
You seem stressed.
First-term nerves?
Starting A levels isn't easy.
I shake my head. *It isn't that . . .*
I hear my voice begin to crack
so I cough instead, then purse my lips
in case any words slip out
that shouldn't. I don't feel like
talking about this now,
I just want to play.
I feel Margaret's green eyes stay
on me, the same way
they did in my first week here,
over three years ago. She
seemed so worried about me,
maybe because Darlington was her idea.

Well, if you ever need to talk, dear,
she says suddenly, *you know where to find me.*
She smiles and frowns at the same time
then moves on briskly.
Let's play some music, shall we?
Who do you want to be today? she asks.
César Franck, Mozart or Bach?
Or how about this beauty,

'The Lark Ascending'?

'The Lark Ascending'

I'd heard it before on the TV

but there's nothing quite like playing

a melody such as this, the solemn ancient promise

of the score, like lines of hieroglyphics, then my fingers

on the strings, reading them aloud like telepathic Braille, while

my arms, body, breath, simultaneously translate it into yet
another language,

that's when you *really* hear it, when it's coming from within
you, travelling through

your ears and out and up,
     disappearing   into the air   like   a bird.

The music brings a memory
Dordogne, France

We hardly went on holiday
but this one Mum won on some website.
It was just a mobile home on a campsite
but when you turned the corner,
  there was paradise.

Fields as far as the eye could see,
bright crowds of sunflowers
bowed in prayer,
and powdered on the lavender sky,
  the blush of sunrise.

Arm wax

Why don't you get your arms waxed?
    Alicia says to me in the study
    as I roll up my shirtsleeves.
I've done mine, see?
Gonna do laser like my mum soon.
    She makes me touch her smooth
    forearm where dark hairs used to be.
    I nearly remember them.
They were as thick as yours, she says.
Now there's nothing,
soft as a baby, she purrs.
You should wax your eyebrows too.
They'd look amazing.

No, thank you, I think.
    Yeah, maybe, I say.

I've got this Arabian friend

      Who says Arabian any more?

      This isn't fucking *Aladdin.*

She's got eyes just like yours,

you should show them off like her,

Layer on that mascara, babes.

       OK, I say, thinking of my mum's

       blue English eyes, of her soft

       blonde arms and legs, never waxed,

       never shaved, how she never

       gave me advice on body hair,

       cos hers is not a bother.

       It's mine that's foreign.

Napping

She's under the covers
her head just visible, bobbing
on a white sea of quilt.
The room is gilt
with the dim light
of that bedside lamp
Mum hates.
I wait until she stirs
before saying a word.

    Mum?
Hmmm?
    Mum, it's me.
Oh, hello, lovely.

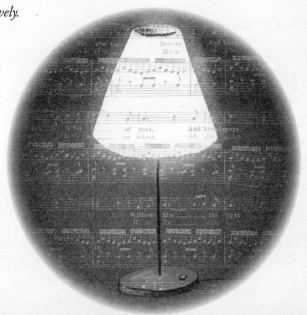

I lie down next to her on the bed.
She turns her head
towards me like a child
and closes her eyes.
I hum her a lullaby,
stroke her hair like she
used to do to me
until she's in
a deep

        deep

                sleep.

Thought while
Mum sleeps

Whenever things at school got tough
     a party I wasn't invited to
     another boy who'd called me rough
Mum would just say *helicopter view*.
This was code for 'close your eyes
and rise up high into the skies'.

I'd see the whole world in my head
and look down at my problems now,
tiny specks, just like she'd said,
and yet it didn't work somehow.
My problems weren't down there below
but inside me, where they could grow.

My only comfort was her voice,
carrying me out of my small room,
the hope there might be an easy choice
to escape my stupid teenage gloom.
I wish I could tell her *helicopter view*,
that now her magic trick was true.

Phoebe's text

Hey you

Watcha up to?

Fancy a visit?

Forgot I've got orthodontist

Right next to yours!

Can I drop in for a cup of chai after?

Emoji heart, choc, poo, laughter

Visitors

I check on Mum to see if she's still asleep,
listening to her breath to hear how deep.

Before, she would have let anyone through
our door, insist on neighbours not
hanging around outside on the path,
invite a mum she just met in the park,
  Come in for a quick cuppa, go on!

Before, she would have fussed about, rushed
to pour Phoebe the juice she kept for guests,
would've filled a plate with home-made cakes,
and quietly slid it to her across the table.
  You need to put on some weight, go on!

But now, she hates people coming round,
especially unannounced. The letter box
makes her jump, the doorbell
makes her run, scuttling to her bedroom
  like a beetle, about to be crushed.

Tidying up

Phoebe's been round countless times
but it doesn't mean I'm not embarrassed by
the size of our house, its tiny patio,
the zero garden, graffiti in our street,
our mismatched crockery,
our one pair of decent dining chairs,

the scratches and tears in the sofa,
thanks to next door's cat,
the petty fact that we only have
a shower and not a bath
because the room is half
the size of The Smallest Bathroom Ever.

So, whenever someone's coming round,
I hoover, mop, dust, rearrange,
polish the picture frames,
wishing that I could push out the walls,
wishing that I could make it all
seem bigger.

The doorbell

Hiya! Phoebe beams, showing off her new brace,
which makes her talk in slurps.
She opens her mouth wide like a vampire
and pulls it out to show me. The plastic bit
that sits against the roof of her mouth is neon pink.
*And get this, the gum he used to make the mould
was watermelon flavour! I love that place.
It's like a space laboratory.*
Phoebe has perfectly straight teeth
except for one at the top which is slightly out of line
but you can only see that when she laughs
and throws her head right back.
Are you gonna invite me in or what?
I forgot, we're still standing on the porch.
            Yeah, sorry, course.
Why are you whispering? Someone asleep?
            Yeah, Mum doesn't feel too well.

This is the moment where I could tell Phoebe
          everything
but I want it all to go away
and words have a way
of making things more true.
Besides, there's nothing she could do.
All this will probably pass in a few weeks.
We'll get her some antidepressants from the GP.
It'll be fine.

        She's got some stomach bug, I lie.

Ugh, Theo had that last week. Thought I'd DIE
when I smelt his bathroom.

Phoebe laughs alone
while I listen to the low
creaks upstairs and Mum
          stopping on the landing.
You OK? Phoebe frowns.
          I point to the ceiling.
          Yeah. I'm just gonna . . . probably
          make her a herbal tea or something.

Shall I go? Phoebe asks
and I know I should say
No, but the thought of
Mum coming down
dishevelled, stern, or even worse,
manic, wide-eyed, asking
weird questions and shit,
makes me just say it.

> *Yeah, maybe? Sorry. Not the best time.*

Sure, fine! Pheebs says brightly,
sweeping a finger
over her phone screen
and ordering an Uber.

Within a minute,
a car pulls up
like some black chariot
and before I know it

> Phoebe's gone.

The next day

Alicia's music's on full blast
    pumping out her Bose Bluetooth speaker, fast,
plosive rapping, thudding bass,
    taking so much space
I can barely think.
    She slinks
across the room
    belting out the tune
making her bum jiggle
    making Phoebe giggle
while her hips curl
    and her hands swirl
above her head, completely
    free.
Could you turn it down a bit?
    I say, feeling my teeth grit.

> *Geez, Grandma, no!*
> *Go to the library, yo!*
What?
> *You heard me. Stop*
> *being such a swot.*
> *You should dance more!*
Alicia tries to pull me onto the floor.
> *Come on, Azzywazzy!*
Don't call me that, please.
> *What's got into you?*
Now Phoebe joins in too.
> *You have been acting pretty weirdly, Az.*
What?
> *You clearly didn't want me round last night.*
Are you serious right now?
> *Yeah, alright, I get your mum had a tummy bug*
> *but even so   Az, don't look at me like that,*
> *you know it's true!*
I feel their eyes burn through me.
How *could* she?

I want to hurl things –
books, pens, those blinging
speakers, Alicia's limbs.
    Even Phoebe.
But instead I hurl half-arsed insults:
You both think you're so adult
just cos you've got money,
everything's funny
to you but you've got no idea
what's real.   Alicia sneers
    Oh, Azadeh, honey.
    You know what's real? MONEY!
    And you should know
    cos you owe
    Phoebe a TON of it.
I turn to Pheebs and she doesn't say shit.
The look in her eyes is enough.
I grab my stuff, swallow my tears
back down into the dark;
hidden
    little
        drops
            of my heart.

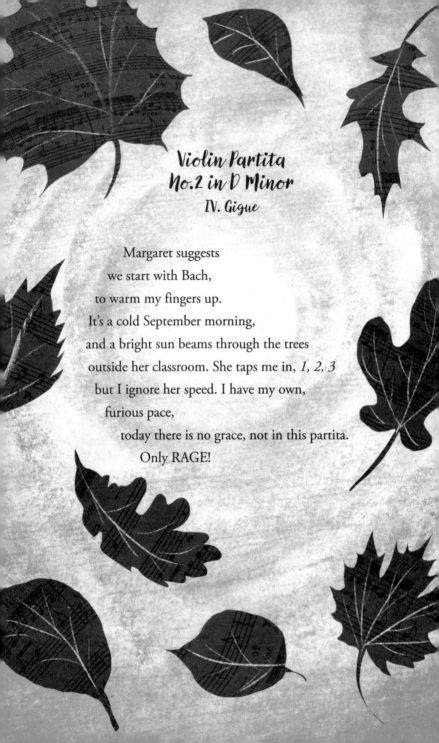

Violin Partita No.2 in D Minor
IV. Gigue

Margaret suggests
we start with Bach,
to warm my fingers up.
It's a cold September morning,
and a bright sun beams through the trees
outside her classroom. She taps me in, *1, 2, 3*
but I ignore her speed. I have my own,
furious pace,
today there is no grace, not in this partita.
Only RAGE!

Orchestra practice

Mr T. has managed to borrow a set of timpani for Jamie,
much to his fury. *Darlington College is made of money!*
A few bloody drums won't break the bank. Music and art
are the heart and soul of this school! he grumbles.

The piece does sound miles better with the rumbling
of the timpani underneath and the gong crashing
and the veins in Jamie's arms flashing,
like blue lightning under his skin.

Visit to Dr Osborne

Mum is furious with me for speaking to *her* GP.
Dad drops us off on his way to work and she sits stonily
in the waiting room, refusing to look at anything,
not even the magazines, not even me.

Katherine Shaw? the receptionist calls, after an eternity.
Mum gets up and so do I but she turns to me quickly,
putting out her arm. *I'm going in alone, please.*
    No-wait-let-me –
You're not my mother, Azadeh. You're sixteen. Now leave!

Prescription

I don't leave. I stay
in the waiting room, listening
to Debussy until Mum reappears.
We get the bus back home in silence.
I watch her folding the doctor's prescription
twice, three times, four, five, like a tight, thick secret.
She holds it for a bit then puts it in her pocket, zips it away.
When we get off, I stop at the pharmacy, but she carries on. *Mum!*
What about your meds? She shakes her head without
turning round, reaches into her pocket
and throws that tiny piece of hope
in the fucking bin.

English homework

This term with Miss Keats
we're doing
Romeo and Juliet
so today she sets
us creative-writing homework
which everyone tries to shirk

> *But, miss!*
> *We can't write this!*
> *It's way too hard!*

Write a poem inspired by the bard
entitled 'What's in a name?'
Choose any poetic frame:
sonnet /haiku /elegy
ghazal/something free
concrete/ekphrastic
make it gymnastic
i.e. bouncing with energy.
Deadline: Friday at three.

Well jel

That evening, when Dad's gone out again,
I think about playing my violin
but I'm so tired I curl up on my bed
and get lost in the Black

               Hole

                   of

                       Instagram.

Phoebe's taken a million selfies
and Alicia's in every single one of them,
  glossy, pouting,
raising her threaded eyebrows
  hashtag birthdaybabes
  hashtag comingsoon
  hashtag fit

hashtag whogivesashit?!

I turn off my phone, toss it
to the other end of the bed
and do my English homework instead.

What's In a Name?

English Creative Writing Assignment   Azadeh Shaw

Shahbazyan: my dad's Persian surname
(large white falcon/heroic, brave)

A rose by any other name would smell as sweet. What's in a name?
My father forgot the Ispahan rose, the perfume contained in a name.

He came to England and his Farsi words fell out of his shallow pockets.
Sounds rolled off his tongue to the floor, like the loose change in a name.

Other words he burned, like cigarettes, then stubbed each one of them out.
The rest blew away on the cold north wind, like the memory in a name.

The English words crept into his thoughts and dreams and so he stayed.
He looked for work, tried to transcribe the reverie in a name.

Still no work, he found himself in the office of deed polls.
A Turkish friend said to anglicise it, for there's Empire in a name.

He was given a list of English names, a civil servant flipped to *Sh*,

Sh, the shushing of his mother, whispering all her desires in a name.

He handed over the ancient bird, too feathered, too heavy now.

Small enough, though, to fit in a drawer, to be filed away in a name.

Shank, Shackle, Shaw, he chose the latter in a matter of minutes.
He didn't know it meant *dweller by the woods*, but dismay can be heard

in a name.

Ali Shaw soon found work, shaved every day to be sure.
Learned a new laugh for English jokes, masked the crying in a name.

Finally he met my mother, who agreed to marry him on one promise,
They'd call their child *Azadeh*. Now *freedom's* flying in a name.

What was Dad thinking?

Shaw is as boring as hell.

I wish I had a Persian surname as well.

    Azadeh Shahbazyan

    AZADEH SHABAZYAN!

At least I'd sound like I'm from Iran.

Maybe I'd feel more whole, more complete,

less of a fraud, less of a cheat,

half one thing, half another,

not quite my father, not quite my mother.

English assignment

Azadeh! Miss Keats says,
spinning my poem through the air
in its protective plastic pocket.
It lands in front of Phoebe, ironically,
two seats away from me.

> We haven't really been speaking
> since the incident in the study.

She looks down at the grade then slides it
across the desk to me, trying to smile
though it looks like more of a wince.

> Nineteen out of twenty, my best mark yet.
> It beats in my chest
> like a proud drum.

Well done! Miss Keats says.
The ghazal is a fantastic form
and of course, being Persian, Azadeh,
you know how to pull it off.
The rhythm must be in your blood!

The letters

Mrs Swift sticks her head round the study door
just before registration.

Azadeh, can I have a quick word? she whispers.
Sure, I say, following her to the office down the corridor.
She shuts the door carefully behind her, motions for me to sit
then settles into her big dusky-pink swivel chair, adjusting
her silk cat-themed scarf before finally looking me in the eye.

So! Azadeh! Everything alright at the moment?
She leans in, puts one hand on her chin, looking teacherly.
What exactly does she mean?
Erm, yeah, yes. I think so. My grades are OK.

Yes, they are . . . OK. She turns to her computer, squints
at the screen.

They're not your usual 'excellent', though. Except for English.
It's true, I haven't handed in any French lately.
And Mr T. basically makes up all our music grades.

But anyway, that's not really my point, Azadeh.
Miss Keats was wondering

                              if everything was alright at home?

Miss Keats?

Yes. You see, she received some letters
from your mother.
My mum?!
    Yes.
What kind of letters?
    I'm not sure exactly. Miss Keats didn't want to
    embarrass you   but she was worried
    about your mother's mental health
    and about you. She asked me to talk to you.

My heart starts pounding fast, sending a dark
rush of adrenalin through my body.
Mrs Swift adjusts her scarf so one of the cats
is suddenly staring straight at me.
If Phoebe were here, it might almost be funny.

She sent actual letters? I ask Mrs Swift, breathlessly.
Addressed to Miss Keats?
Mrs Swift raises one neat
drawn-on eyebrow.
    Yes, it is quite unusual.
She has a knack for putting a mild spin
on everything.

OK, I see, I say, trying to sound cool,
like I'm just talking about a pet.
Mrs Swift would actually make a good vet –
    much better than a housemistress.
Well, yes, my mum has been a bit
    off, not sleeping properly.
We think it's due to hormones.
She's been to see the GP though
and it's all   under control.

I smile at Mrs Swift, give her the reassurance she needs
to leave me alone. Meanwhile on the inside
    I am mortified.

WTF?

What was in the letters, Mum?

She's at the kitchen table, head in her hands,
her hair hanging lankly around her face,
papers spilling all over the place.

Hang on, Az, I need to concentrate.
This is very important.

> *THIS is more important.*
> *I hear you sent letters to Miss Keats?*

Hmm? Who?

> *My English teacher!* I say impatiently.
> Don't tell me she can't even remember her name now.
Eye-roll emoji!

Oh yes, I remember, she says casually.
I only wrote a few.

> *But why?! Why did you   do that?*

Don't get all aggressive now, Azadeh.
You really need to control your temper.
You get that from your dad.

    WHAT?

Oh yes, he might seem all mild-mannered
but you've never seen him get really
angry, like I have.

    STOP! I don't want to hear this, Mum!
    You're talking nonsense, you're not right in the head.
    I want to know exactly what you said
    to MY teacher! I have the right to know!

You're blowing it all out of proportion, Azadeh.

    I hate the way she uses my full name whenever she's
    trying to show she's more in control than me.

I merely wrote to say how much I admired her CV.
I looked it up on the school website.
You know that she writes too?
I told her I'm finishing my autobiography and asked
if she'd look at a first draft,
when it's ready, obviously.

Oh. My. GOD. Mum!
You're doing my head in!
Can't you see that's a weird thing to do?!

Weird for who? You really need to
get over yourself, Azadeh. Maybe
think more about these refugees,
struggling to survive. That's real plight.

Nice letters to your teacher are no big deal!

English class

I think about skipping my next English class.
I could fill in a music-lesson excusal slip
and put it in Miss Keats's pigeon hole, but it's risky.
I don't want Mrs Swift calling me back in,
so I go, pretend everything's perfectly alright,
try not to think about what ravings might
or might not be in those letters,
smile as brightly as I can to prove
to Miss Keats that
my mother is not mad,
my mother is NOT mad,
MY MOTHER IS NOT MAD!

Miss Keats told us

> *there is nothing either good or bad,*
> *but thinking makes it so.*

I wrote these words on my folder in bright blue.
Shakespeare, Hamlet, Act II, scene ii.

Later I repeat them to myself,
feeling their rhythm in my feet,
their metre in my heels
as they hit the pavement home.

> *There is nothing either good or bad,*
> *but thinking makes it so.*

Money

That afternoon, Dad's at home,
clutching papers, on the phone.
Mum's been spending like there's no
tomorrow,
as if money grows on trees,
trying to save her refugees,
and now we're strapped
for cash
a light purse
heavy curse
in the red
an arm and a leg
barely keeping

         our heads

              above

                    water.

Days

Mum lets the days
slip away
ignores
the friends who call
and Aunty Fay
who wants to stay
next week

No one
says Mum
No one
No one

No one

Busking

The first weekend without rain in weeks,
just a plain grey sheet for a sky.
I take my violin, go into town
and play to the trickling crowds
that gather and pass like clouds,
moving in the wind, moving to my tune.
A girl with a moon-like face
empties all her change into my case
from a furry unicorn purse, asks
for her favourite Disney songs,
which then attract throngs
of kids dragging parents, dropping in pounds,
coins that land with a different sound,
     shiny, clinking music to my ears!

Saturday night

Tamsin seems to be
the only one messaging me.
I think she feels sorry
for me or something.
I mean, we were never super close
but she's kinder than most.
She texts me,

> *We're at some random's house party.*
> *Actually fun! Come!*

I think about staying in with Mum
but it doesn't ever seem
to do any good, plus I'm keen
to get out
of the house,
lose myself in a crushing crowd,
drown my thoughts in loud
music and shouting conversations
before I start to go crazy
myself.

House party

Is it weird to say I can sense
Phoebe's presence
in a room, before I've even
seen her? Like telepathy
or something equally freaky.
Like now, I know she hasn't arrived
so I don't have to hide
just yet, but I check anyway.
      I was right. She's always late.

Half the sixth form is here,
including Jamie Weir.
           Azadeh! he says, as our eyes
              awkwardly meet. *Hey!*
He knows my name?!
           Didn't bring your violin? He grins.
It's in my handbag. Hang on . . .
Hope you've got your drums?!

Jamie starts doing an impression of Mr T.
waving his arms around wildly.

> *Come ON, timpani!*
> *1, 2, 3 . . .*

That actually sounds like him! I laugh
and Jamie shyly rubs the stubble on his chin.

> *Thanks! Seriously though,*
> *I don't know how I got roped*
> *into any of it.*
> *I am NO percussionist!*
> *I play rock, punk, drum 'n' bass,*
> *for God's sake! Not classical!*

But you're doing SO great!
Why does my voice sound so fake?
Cringe!

Jamie's not normally my type
but his brown eyes are so big and kind
and after I've downed my wine
he is suddenly   super fine.

We carry on talking about orchestra
and I'm aware of all the eyes in the room
but I don't care because something blooms
inside me that isn't gloom
for once. A rush
in my blood, a flush
in my cheeks.
>   *Hey, let me*
>   *get you another drink.*
No need, I say, *I'm good!*

I'm actually more than good.
I want to stay exactly like this,
both of us *just-turned-tipsy-grinning*
not *drunk-shit-oh-now-the-room's-spinning*.

For once in a long time, I want to remember everything.

Pre-kiss worry

How do you know if you're a good kisser?

The last guy I kissed was Martin Luck,
and it was like having my tongue stuck
in a washing machine
on a fast spin,
thrusting round and round,
could barely breathe.

Then he said to his friends
that I was the one
who was the washing machine!

It's like dancing though.
He led, so

        my tongue just

                followed.

Kiss

I could tell by the way
his head came
towards me
the way his lips parted slowly
that this
would be a good kiss.

There were no washing machines here,
no fear
of thrusting tongues
or bursting lungs,
there was no need
to lead.

Our mouths just
    met
    warm and wet
and became one dark space
        a place
           to explore
      be lost
        tossed on a wave
              of bliss

Yes, this
is what a good kiss
is.

Going . . .

I decide to go on a high note
in spite of Jamie's attempts to persuade me to stay.
I slip away and leave him air-drumming
on the kitchen floor. I wish I could stay a bit more
but Dad's outside, waiting for me.
I told him I'd get a taxi, then he tried to make me agree
to a pick-up round the corner at ten.
WAY too early, Dad!
            OK, eleven then.
Fine. But I don't know why you won't
just let me get an Uber.
            It's dangerous on Saturday night.
Ubers aren't dangerous, Dad.
They've got driver ratings.
And you can trace the number plate.
It's really safe.
            Ha – safe!
            Nothing's safe these days, Azadeh!
            You must
            trust no one!

...Going...

I see Phoebe on my way out,

looking even more gorgeous than usual.

She's as good at applying eye make-up as she is paint,

same bright colours too, her faves,

tropical blue, fluorescent pink,

a hint of gold on the bones of her cheeks.

I sneak out before she sees me,

before this heady feeling leaves me,

before I forget how much it meant

to be kissed tonight.

. . . Gone

I crunch six Tic Tacs, spray perfume
to mask the smell of Jamie-plus-booze,
though surely Dad's no fool,
he knows what we get up to.
There are just three silent rules:
>Don't have sex
>Don't come home blind drunk
>Never, ever take drugs.

Good night? he asks as I get in the van,
slamming the door safely shut.
>*Yeah, guess so.* I shrug,
not letting on just how much
it was
>a really
>>good
>>>night.

Home

I check on Mum, she's fast asleep.
I think she better today, Dad says.
She even went to get her meds.
Must admit, that was quite a relief.

Tidying

Mum's up first thing,
at the sink, wringing
out the dishcloth, cleaning
the kitchen surfaces, polishing
the drawer handles, scrubbing
the gas rings.
I wasn't sleeping,
no point tossing and turning.
She starts rearranging
the Tupperware drawer, putting
lids on the right boxes, rinsing
ones that already look clean to me,
folding tea towels, hiding
them in drawers, thinking, thinking
about something.
Maybe this is the meds, the beginning
of her getting up, getting out, getting
better   or maybe this isn't anything
and I'm clinging
to my own

        dwindling

                hope.

Lesson with Margaret

When I play
Margaret always has something to say,
a crescendo here, a breath there,
tilt the hair
of your bow!
Your violin's too low!
Keep your back straight!
Put more weight
into the bowing arm!
Now keep it light!
Fingers too tight!
Tempo too slow!
More legato!
Use the lower half of the bow!
Lift your elbow!
Lift, lift!
(you catch my drift)

but today
Margaret says
nothing.

Impressed

You've been practising
          more than usual.
She smiles. *I can tell.*
          Four hours a day, I say.
Well, well, well.

Break time

I spy the top of Jamie's curly head
at the other end of the corridor,
like he's countries away.

Morning, earthling! He winks
as we finally cross paths.
See you on Mars!
I smile back and feel
El's eyes rolling at me.

Ugh, I can't BELIEVE
you snogged him, Azzy.
He's not even that fit.
Plus you must be THE
most unlikely couple!

What's that supposed to mean?

It means he's into rich blonde girls.

I see, so basically
girls that are nothing like me.

No! I just mean that he's slightly
shallow.

> *El, YOU'RE rich and blonde!*
> *And so is Phoebe!*
> *So are most of the cool*
> *girls in this school!*
> *Does that make you all shallow?*
> *Does that make everyone who's into you shallow?*

Oh stop it, Azzy. No, of course not!
I just think you're too
good for him, that's all.

I don't bother replying.
I'm in too good a mood
to let El's jealousy
get under my skin.
She's blatantly in the dumps
cos she hasn't pulled in months.

Anyway, who cares who Jamie's
usually into? I'm going to enjoy him being into me.

The end of the day

It's one of those fiery sunsets,
darkening skies, clouds a-smoking
and Dad's van is there, the engine choking,
waiting for me
though he's not meant to be.

I pray he's just finished early
and thought I might like a lift back
seeing as the buses are crap,
like he'd sometimes do,
once in a blue moon.

But I know from the roaring silence
as I get in, his hug a second too long,
I know that something's really wrong,
so wrong he has to do small talk first,
else he'll burst.

It's not till we get to the coast road
that he tells me we're not going home.
We drive past crashing waves, all foam,
and I see his face, like a crumpled map,
one hand trembling in his lap.

Mum's taken an overdose,
I hear him say.
But she's OK.

He means alive-OK
cos she can't really be OK
no way, no way,
I think
as I watch the day　　sink

　　　　deeply

　　　　devastatingly

　　　　into

　　　　the sea.

Crushed

She crushed them up one by one,
pill
after
pill.

Dad says she lost her
will,
she's ill.
But still.

I wonder how many pills
will
kill
a mother?

And did she know
when
to
stop?

And will
she kill
herself
again?

And will
I ever
be
enough?

Skyline

Far away
the hospital stands out against the night sky,
tall like a lighthouse, bright
like a Christmas tree,
but when we wind up
to the top of the hill and get up close, it's as tall as the dark,
as bright as fire,
and I'm
frightened
of what
I will
find
there.

Not happening

We swish through the doors of A&E
and I imagine in my head this is just TV,
just another episode of *Casualty*,
that this woman's blood is ketchup,
that man's bruised face is make-up
and all these doctors and nurses
are just pretending to be this serious.

Haunting corridors

Dad is trailing behind me
like a shadow
or a ghost
or a shadow of a ghost.

At the desk, I say her name
which is my name too
which is my pain too,
sticking in my throat
like tonsillitis.

They tell us what her ward
is called
and that's that,
they don't give you a map,
you have to figure this out alone,
read the writing on the walls,
pass through automatic doors
that creak like old bones,
go down corridors that split like veins,
ride in lifts that smell the same
        as death probably does.

Hospital Mum

I find her behind a hospital curtain
in a hospital bed
in hospital sheets
in a hospital gown
in hospital skin
with a hospital face
and hospital hair

Hospital
hospital
hospital
hospital
hospital
hospital
Mum.

She manages to say two words

Sorry
Love.

Cut

Mum once told me
your brain
forgets pain.
The worst kind, anyway.

She said, *It's easy to remember*
    what a cut
    or sting is like
but it's hard to remember
    just how bad earache is
    or birth pains
    or worse, toothache.

Toothache,
which makes you
want to yank out every single one of your teeth
and never eat again,
toothache that spreads
through your head,
makes you almost
wish you were dead.

That was
my worst kind of pain,
until now.

Now, there is This Pain
that is like
every pain added together since the day I was born,
screaming my way out of her

. . .

. . .

. . .

. . .

. . .

So painful
I cut it out of my memory
I cut it out of this poem

(cut to next poem)

Takeaway

When we come away
we don't say anything
but Dad stops the van at the Indian place
and orders everything I like,
even the expensive starters
and a Cobra beer each.

We eat it from the tinfoil boxes
and turn on the TV
because Mum isn't here to tell us off
and now is really not the time
to have *nice family chats*.

I dip my poppadoms
in mango chutney
and yoghurt sauce
and that spicy lime pickle I love,
sink my teeth
into the sweet stuffing
of a peshwari naan soaked
in chicken tikka masala sauce.

And I thank the God of Indian Food
that for these few minutes,
we're OK.

Night without Mum

When the food has gone
and the tinfoil boxes
are crushed in the bin,

when the TV's off,
front door's locked
and there's nothing but
the hushed
tick of the clock
and, far off,
the faint roar
of Dad's snores,

that's when the night pours in.

Dream funeral

I dream that Mum
did die
and the dread
of her dying
is dead with her too,
lowered
into
a
hole
in a casket big enough for the three of us.

When I wake up and realise it's not real
I feel weirdly angry

angry that I cannot mourn her death
when it feels like she's already died

angry that I should really be happy
my mum's still alive

angry that she wanted to leave me
behind.

Sick note

Dad wants me to take the day off.
He says he'll write me a sick note,
but there's nothing I can do at home
and visiting hours aren't till the afternoon.
If Dad's going to work, I'm carrying on too.
But could you write me a note
to get me off sport? I ask.
I don't have the heart
to fart around
in a netball skirt right now.

Forgetting

Routine is a precious thing,
    I clasp it like a prayer.
Wake, shower, dress, hair,
    eat, leave, leaving . . .

Everything seems as before,
    bus, assembly, file, rank.
Memory's something that I drank
    for breakfast this morning.

Mrs Swift

Mrs Swift waits for me outside Chapel,
takes me gently aside. *I got your dad's note, Azadeh.*
I'm so sorry to hear your mum's in hospital.
What happened exactly? Is she alright?

We are alone now but it suddenly feels like
the whole school might be listening.
So I play it down, shrink it, crush it, hoping that way
it'll all just go away.

> *Yes, she's alright*
> *just exhausted, mentally.*

I don't mention A&E.
Dad's note didn't either – I checked, obviously.

Right, yes, of course, of course she must be. Mrs Swift sighs,
shaking her head the way a concerned adult's supposed to.
You said she hadn't been quite herself.
Well, at least she's resting now, and
in good hands, getting the right treatment.
As long as you're alright?

I'm fine. I smile.

*Well, you know where I am
if you need me, Azadeh.*

Yes, thank you, miss.

She nods sympathetically
and I'm dismissed.

Secret

I'm all poker face,
my lips are sealed,
I'm biting my tongue,
I'm a cat in the bag,
as quiet as a mouse,
a dark horse.
I'm a thief in the night,
behind closed doors,
keeping everyone in the dark,
    including myself.
I cover my tracks,
don't crack,
don't dish the dirt,
won't take the lid off
and spill the beans,
won't leak, won't speak,
keep it under my hat,
under wraps.
I'll keep a low profile,
won't give the game away,
won't say   anything
cos Mum's the word.

Lesson with Margaret

Margaret is all bunged up
and spends the entire hour
sniffing, sneezing, apologising,
blowing her nose with gusto
like a Mozart trumpet fanfare.

But I'm relieved
that her ears are all clogged up
and for once she cannot hear
that I'm out of tune
or notice me stooping,
drooping over my violin,

                        like a wilting

                                  flower.

The Madhouse

I take a bus I've never been on
in the opposite direction to
everywhere I know, to just before
the greyhound stadium,
where the dogs whimper in cages.

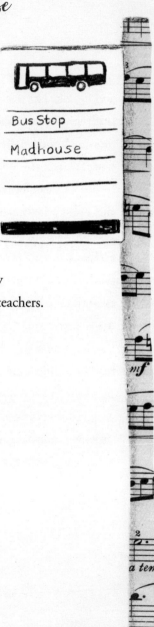

In primary school, we called it
The Madhouse,
put every terrifying person in there,
the graveyard drunks, that wailing lady
in the high street, most of our supply teachers.

I get up to press the bell
and look at who else is on this bus.
Don't want anyone I know to see me
getting off at The Madhouse stop.

Seaview Clinic

There's no sea or view
and it looks like one of those new
hotels on the motorway, Holiday Inn
or something equally disappointing.

Inside it's clean like bleach
and I pass a room where people eat
grey food off grey trays.
Others wander the corridors like stray
cats, glassy-eyed, skin the colour of stone,
either bloated or all bone.

I go up the stairs to Nightingale Ward,
hoping to find a kindly nurse called
Florence, or some singing birds,
but there's no music here, just jumbled words,
shrieking, moaning, swearing.
Someone pleading, a TV blaring.

Bird Mum

I find her in her room, sitting on the edge of a bed,
drugged up to her translucent blue
eyeballs. *How are you, love?*
she coos like a wounded dove.

We hug, and there are parts of her that stick into me
where flesh used to be.

Everything reeks of medication, except her hair,
which smells unwashed but I don't care
because at least that's human,
     it's better than nothing.

The psychiatrist

The doctor
in charge of Mum
sits me down
and I think
he's going to explain
what's going on
shed some light
on all this dark,
his white coat bright
at the end
of this tunnel
but instead
he pummels my head
with questions.

When did she
What did she
Why did she
Why did you
Why didn't you
How did you
How did she
How come she

How come
you're such
a dick?

After . . .

I run to my room and close the door
and cry like I've never cried before,
like my insides are pouring out.

I want to scream and shout
but Dad's downstairs so I do that silent crying
that's even worse   like slowly dying

from a shuddering sadness

or a kind of madness.

When I go to play . . .

I open my case
and my violin suddenly
reminds me of a body,
sunk in a felt-lined coffin,
a limbless trunk,
a shrunken neck,
a freaky tiny scroll head.
I close the case again,
snap it shut,
zip it up,

so

no

ghosts can

escape.

Days

Days go by without me
playing, without me
saying anything,
and all these woven parts of me
start to fray.

Techniques for avoiding everyone at school

1   I take the bus after eight,
     which makes me two minutes late
     for registration, so I have to go straight
     to Chapel, for assembly, alone.

2   Morning break, lunchtime, afternoon,
     I take refuge in the music school,
     entombed, enwombed in a practice room,
     tuning myself into another world.

3   In class I go in last, sit apart,
     don't ask or answer questions, glance up
     only if I have to, so this mask
     of mine never

                  ever

                          falls.

English class

Azadeh? Miss Keats calls after class.

I'm halfway down the corridor,
moving fast.

Can I have a word?

I can't be arsed with pity right now
but I follow her to the staffroom anyway.

Are you OK? she asks.

I'm fed up of that question. Pass.

Mrs Swift told me about your mum being ill.
I'm sorry about mentioning the letters. I didn't want to
embarrass you. Not that there's anything
to be embarrassed about.

Miss Keats's milky cheeks flush a painful pink
like she's suddenly been slapped.
She tucks her neat black bob behind her ears.

Sure. I nod. *I get it.*

> *Anyway, I just wanted to give you a heads-up*
> *that we'll be doing John Clare next lesson.*
> *You know, the poet? Because he had*
> *mental health difficulties too.*
> *I just want to make sure it's not too much for you?*

I don't really get it but I appreciate the gesture.
Yes, it's fine, miss. I shrug.   *Whatever.*

Missed calls

Recent

Phoebe	15.03
Phoebe	15.05
Phoebe	15.08
Phoebe	15.09

Texts from Phoebe

Azzy you OK?

Mrs Swift just told me your mum's in hospital.

Hope everything's alright. Call me.

Where are you?

Why is your stuff here but you're not at school?

Bunking off

I dump my bag in the study
                    and run

                              run

                                        down to the sea.

I sit on stones
              as close to the water

                          as the raging waves

                                        will allow me.

Not so long ago
                we came as a family,

                          throwing stones

                                        as far as we could see.

Me with weakling arms
                    and Dad who used to be

                              so strong

                                        and Mum, laughing.

The next day

The buses are on strike
so Dad is taking me,
though admittedly
I'd prefer the nine-mile walk.
We don't talk
the whole way there,
barely breathing the same air,
and when we approach the gates
I'm expecting him to slow down, wait
for me to actually get out.
Dad, what are you DOING? I shout.
Next thing I know
he's speeding up, all gung-ho,
driving his van through those bloody
arches for everyone to see.

Argument

What are you DOING?! I shout again.

Can't you see?
I take my daughter to her fancy
school. Shamelessly. Proudly.
These are words you really
need to learn again, Azadeh.

I get out, slam the door, not daring
to look up and see who's staring.
Like I'm going to take a lesson
in learning words from *him!*

You forgot your violin,
he says calmly, rolling
the window down.

I'm done with all that now,
I don't need it.

Why don't YOU keep it?!

211

Now I dare to look

And who do I see?
Jamie, obviously,
now awkwardly pretending
to check his Mini
but clearly he's seen everything.

> *Oh, hey, Azzy!* he says coolly.
> *What's up?*

I want the ground to swallow me up,
that's what.

Oh, hi, Jamie.

> *Not seen you at orchestra lately.*

No. I've been off sick, I lie.
Would he have checked up on me?
I seriously
doubt it.

So you're not avoiding me?
                    Cos of the other night.

I've got a lot going on, alright?
The words come out sharper than I meant
and he gives me this dented smile.

                    See you around then.

Yeah.

'I Am'
by John Clare

I am – yet what I am none cares or knows;
My friends forsake me like a memory lost:
I am the self-consumer of my woes –
They rise and vanish in oblivious host,
Like shadows in love's frenzied stifled throes
And yet I am, and live – like vapours tossed

Into the nothingness of scorn and noise,
Into the living sea of waking dreams,
Where there is neither sense of life or joys,
But the vast shipwreck of my life's esteems;
Even the dearest that I loved the best
Are strange – nay, rather, stranger than the rest.

I long for scenes where man hath never trod
A place where woman never smiled or wept
There to abide with my Creator, God,
And sleep as I in childhood sweetly slept,
Untroubling and untroubled where I lie
The grass below – above the vaulted sky.

Keys

Miss Keats was right,
it is too much,
I'm trying to shut
the door
but some poems are
master keys,
slipping through

the

stiff

lock

of

my

soul.

Answerphone

You have
one message.
Message one.

> Hello, Azadeh dear,
> Margaret here.
> I just wanted to see if you're alright.
> It's most unlike
> you to miss a lesson
> though perhaps you just forgot.
> Anyhow, it's not
> too late to come,
> if you get this
> before half six.
> Just let me know.
> Cheerio now.

Dad tells me

You do violin practice after dinner, OK?
                    Since when do you start telling me
                            when to practise, hey?
Since now, I start.
Since I hear nothing for weeks.
Since you do not even speak.
Since our house feels like empty heart.

Walk

I need to get out of there, get away
from Dad breathing down my neck every second of the day,
from everyone at school asking if I'm OK,
so I walk and walk, until the streets all look the same.

Eventually I start to cross the bridge over the motorway
and stop halfway,
                  take in the indifference of concrete,
and traffic, rumbling thunderous beneath my feet,
the cars streaming, streaming, like tears.

And then dark thoughts creep in.

I wonder what it would be like to fall.

I wonder if Mum considered other sorts of death at all.

I wonder if one day I

might also want to die.

Azadeh

AZADEH!

AZADEH!

It's Dad, running across the bridge.

GET AWAY FROM THERE!

I take a step back, even though I'm nowhere
near the barrier.

WHAT YOU DOING, EH?!

What are YOU doing, you mean?
I wasn't gonna jump, you know!

Why you walk out like that?

Stop SHOUTING, it's embarrassing!
People in their cars are looking!
You look like a complete WEIRDO.

> *We going home.*
> *You don't do that to me again,*
> *you hear me, young lady?*

> **You DON'T do that**
> **ever again!**

Persian stew

When we get back to our empty house, Dad clatters around
in the kitchen taking out every pot and pan,
                banging something with a rolling pin.

Soon, the earthy smell of walnuts toasting travels through
the rooms.
I spy Dad making my favourite meal,
                fesenjoon.

The ground walnuts look like sugar now, crumbly,
golden bright.
Dad pours on water, lets it simmer to a paste,
                clamps the lid on tight.

He fries onion and big strips of chicken breast, pours on
the nutty paste,
mixes in pomegranate juice, sprinkles its seeds
                then finally tastes.

It really needs golden plums. He frowns, serving me some
saffron rice.

He spoons on the rich, red-brown sauce. I try it.

No. It's nice.

But it's more than nice, so much more. It's so delicious
I'm nearly in tears.

I can see why Persians have eaten this dish for thousands
and thousands of years.

Dream

please fit your fingers in mine
please sing into my ear
please whisper me all those stories
please stay with me right here

please caress my cheek
please stroke that bit of my brow
please wrap me up inside you
please Mum hold me now

Decision

As I wake up, I have this tune turning round in my head,
turning round in my head, I have this tune, as I wake up.

I've no idea what I dreamt, except for this melody,
except for this melody, I've no idea what I dreamt.

It feels like this was its soundtrack, on a loop, all night,
all night, on a loop, it feels like this was its soundtrack.

The title comes back to me, *Spiegel im Spiegel*, mirror in mirror,
mirror in mirror, *Spiegel im Spiegel*, the title comes back to me.

I want to see Margaret again, hold my violin, make music,
make music, hold my violin, I want to see Margaret again.

Facing the music

I've skipped three weeks of lessons.
The first two, I told Margaret I was sick,
the third that I was on a trip.
She probably checked up, found me out,
but she doesn't say anything now,
    she simply lets me play.

I choose an old piece, just to be safe,
Beethoven Sonata No. 5, Spring,
but immediately my fingers are tensing
and I'm fluffing all the notes,
    stopping
            and starting
       chopping
            and carving
    up the rhythm

but if there's anything Margaret's taught me
it's to keep on bashing through it
and so I massacre the piece
to the very
           end.

Margaret's hug

She waits until the echo
of our last notes together have faded
then she gets up from her piano stool
and hugs me.

I want to hug her back
but my violin's in one hand,
my bow in the other
so I just let myself be hugged

a hug as soft as Debussy
as warm as Bach
as floral as Schumann
as memorable as Mozart

and suddenly I'm crying,
a shuddering cry
like every pore of my skin
is weeping
and something like grief
seeps out of me.

I tell her everything

As much as I can anyway,
      between all the blubbering
and spitting out bits of sentences, as if
      a boa constrictor's
                        twisting itself
            around
                  my neck.

            It's OK, Margaret says. *It's OK, just let it all out.*
            Then she takes my violin from me,
            places it in its soft case, carefully,
            as if she's putting a baby to sleep.

It's all my fault! I hear myself say, breathlessly,
the words choking me.
It's all my fault!
      It's all my fault!
                  IT'S
                              ALL
                                    MY
                                          FAULT!

230

Wisdom

We sit down side by side
and after I've wiped away all my snot
Margaret speaks even slower than usual,
as if she's plucking words
out of the universe.

> *Azadeh,*
> *none of this is your fault –*
> *what's happening to your mum,*
> *it's called a nervous breakdown*
> *and it can happen to anyone.*
> *She did not want to die.*
> *She did not want to leave you,*
> *Azadeh.*
> *She wanted to leave her mind,*
> *her condition.*
> *She doesn't love you any less.*
> *Do you understand,*
> *Azadeh?*

I nod, the tears streaming by themselves now.
I let them fall between my feet, watch them form
a tiny lake I wish I were small enough to drown in.
Margaret interrupts the thought
with words that shimmer in the dark:

You're never alone, dear,
not when you have music.

Diagnosis

I don't know if it is a diagnosis
but it's the first time anyone has given me
a way to name it.

Nervous breakdown.

It is mechanical, mildly medical,
better than madness anyway. I take it, gratefully,
hoping it's as fixable as it sounds.

Margaret's solution

Which hospital is your mother at, dear?
I tell her and she nods knowingly.
Well, when you next pay her a visit
take her some music.
She scrawls on a musical Post-it.
This should do the trick.

Prescription for depression

Bach's Italian Concerto in F major
Corelli's Concerto grosso in D major, Op. 6, No. 4
Mozart's Sonata for Two Pianos in D major, K.448

To be taken one hour per day   for at least eight weeks

Texting Phoebe

Hi

I'm sorry

> Hi

> Me too
> Do you wanna talk about it?

No not really

> Is she OK?

She's fine

I hate that word,
wrapping around me like twine,
fine, fine, fine
it means
nothing

> Shall we talk at break?

Yeah.

That'd be great.

Break

It's impossible to find
somewhere quiet
in our school.
The sixth form cafe's
full of the usual
couples, drooling
over each other,
and in the computer room
there's Jamie, who
I really want to talk to,

    just not now,

so I drag Phoebe out
before he turns around
and sees me.

We try the library,
but it's so silent
our whispers are crisp
as crackling leaves
in a forest.
It's best we go
down the road,
I say.
This way,
towards the sea,
and slowly,
like I'm unravelling
a reel of thin thread,
   the kind that, wound too tight,
         can cut into
               your skin,

I tell
Phoebe everything.

The truth

I wrap up the truth in soft words
like tissue paper, almost translucent,
susceptible to creases and tears
but prettier, like Phoebe.

Words like   *unwell*   *not herself*
just a few pills   *a cry for help*
I say *she's in the hospital for a bit*
but do not say which one.

When I finish and the words hang awkwardly
on the air, like fog over the sea,

                              me and Phoebe hug
                              a long, sorry embrace
then we sit, displacing the mound of pebbles,
which crunch under our weight,
our backs hunched against the wind,
our arms huddled together
to weather the cold air and the spitting sea.

We build a pile of stones the way Dad taught me,
hit them with bigger rocks until they topple.

That is A LOT of shit, Phoebe says,
still solemnly hitting the fallen stones.

I knew she'd be all quiet like this.
She prefers to dismiss pain,
never knowing quite what to say.

I look at her frowning face
and suddenly wish I could take
all of my words back, unload the weight
I've put on her graceful shoulders.

I want to be the friend who lifts her up
not pulls her d

        o

        w

        n.

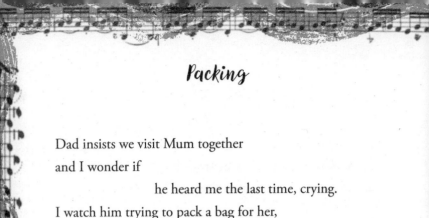

Packing

Dad insists we visit Mum together
and I wonder if
                        he heard me the last time, crying.
I watch him trying to pack a bag for her,
hovering in front of her side of the wardrobe,
plucking out random things he thinks she likes,
holding up bright shirts and smart trousers
she hasn't worn in months.

Here, I'll finish the rest, I say, finding
her comfy pants, her favourite stripy tops.
I slip in some poetry books too
and a few photos in frames,
hoping to make her hospital room less sterile,
even if it is only for a while.

    At least, that's what I hope.

Visit to Mum

When we enter her room, we can smell
the remains of dinner, ratatouille with rice.
I see Mum's eaten most of it, and the smell
suddenly makes me swell with hope.

She gets up to hug me this time.
    Hello, love. I saved you some pud.
I don't feel like chocolate mousse
but I take it anyway. *Thanks*, I say,
and Mum sits down, relieved,
as if she made the mousse herself.

She watches me eat while Dad asks questions
I'm not sure he really wants the answers to.

    What time did you have lunch?
    What film they putting on?
    Where have all your grapes gone?

I think he just wants to keep her talking,
pedalling endless questions, keeping
the dynamo light in her eyes flickering,
as if this exchange of words will keep her alive.

I start putting things we brought her onto the shelves.
I'm not moving in, she says as I delve into the bag
and pull out the photo frames.
She tries to sound jokey but it comes out strained.

    I know. I smile. *I just thought*
    cos they don't let you use your phone much,
    you might like pictures of us.

I suddenly remember my iPod and rummage in my bag.

I've downloaded some music for you, Mum.

Listen to the first playlist — an hour a day, if you can.

Mum takes it and stares at the tangled headphones.

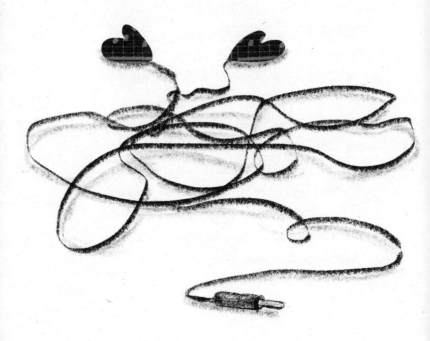

Thank you, love, she whispers.

I'll try my best.

Desert

Dad's work really has dried up now.
The guy with the flats in town
found an electrician
who could work much quicker.

Dad's trying to play it down but I see him
frowning at the bills, hear him
phoning up old contacts,
selling himself cheap to big building sites

and then calling up his bank
to convince them
in his nicest English
to give him a bigger overdraft

and the sinking tone
of his voice
when they
don't.

Phoebe's texts

Come out with us tonight, Az! Please!
We're going to Freeze
It's hip-hop night!
Jamie might
even be there, you never know!

No, you guys go.
I won't be very
good company

Azzy!
You shouldn't be
on your own,
not at the moment!

Pub again

After dinner, Dad disappears
for the fourth time this week.
He says he's taking the recycling to the bins
out on the main road, *the long way round*
so my food digests.

But I always smell the beer on his breath
as soon as he steps through the door.

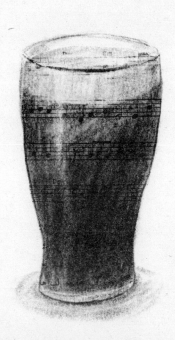

World Wide Web

While Dad is out I suddenly have an idea
and open up my laptop,
tap Dad's website in the search bar

www.alishawelectrics.com

He hasn't updated it for at least three years
and the logo he paid our neighbour's son to do
really sucks. I open up a Word doc
and start clicking shapes and text into place,
a lightbulb here, a few stars there.
I export, upload, update,
then create new pages.

> *About. Prices. Contact.*
> *Customer Reviews* (OK, I made a few of them up)
> *and . . . Publish!*

When that's finished, I get onto Google Business
and every forum out there, spreading the word,

**Excellent Expert
Electrician
No job too small!**

Lesson with Margaret

Today, Margaret is watching me differently,
listening intently, as if I'm playing in a new language.
She makes small adjustments to my posture,
    the gentlest tap on the shoulder to relax
    or straighten my back,
but otherwise she does not interrupt,
just nods at every phrase,
agreeing with everything my violin says.

Playing 'The Lark Ascending'

In a matter of moments, it's as if
the earth knits itself back together again,
the wretched chasm closes over,
heals as miraculously as skin. It's as if

the thrashing temper of the sea, rolling
in on itself, frothing, spewing stones, suddenly
gives up and withdraws, its roars diminishing
to the whispering of foam. It's as if

a tiny light appears in all this darkness,
a faint, flickering star
quietly reminding me that there is
something far, far beyond it.

A proposition

I have an idea, Margaret says. *Now do not feel obliged, dear,*
but there's a Christmas concert I'm conducting
with the county orchestra. Our soloist just dropped out.
But I was thinking you could do 'The Lark'!
The orchestra's done it before, on tour,
and you play it so sensationally!
It's in only three weeks
but you're already ready, dear,
*   very ready.*

Yes!

When I get back home
I practise, practise like mad,
just like I used to whenever I had
grade exams, concerts, competitions.
     Margaret calls it
     practising with a mission!
And when my arms ache,
and my fingers nearly break,
I collapse onto my bed,
burying my head
in YouTube videos
of every soloist
who ever played
'The Lark Ascending',
          eventually
              descending
                    into a deep
                        and peaceful
                            sleep.

Work at last

Dad gets off the phone and his lips
break into a gentle smile.
*Looks like your Internet work
paying off.
Want to earn another bob?*

 You got a job?! I say.

He nods. *Whole house rewire,
start this weekend.
I need assistant though,
lift floorboard, chase wire,
you know, keep place tidy.
I'll pay you well.* He winks.
I think about it for all of one second.

 Yeah, go on then!

Hard work

I knew Dad worked hard but I didn't know
it would make my whole body ache,
that there'd be hours of crouching, squatting, lifting,
with dust sifting on my head
and the owner's cat clambering up my leg.
  You take break, he says, popping another
  Nicorette gum out of the blister pack.
I watch him chew it fast, like a hamster.
You know you can smoke in front of me,
I say eventually.
He shakes his head. *No, this time
I've given up for good.*

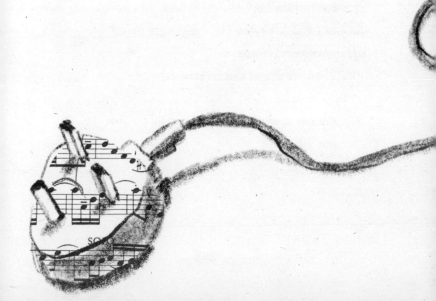

Lunch

We forge on all morning
not stopping for a minute not even
to check my phone,
until Dad checks his watch

    never his hunger
to see if it's time for lunch.
12:30. Let's eat.
He brushes himself down,
washes his hands, scrubs his nails clean.

He takes out our packed lunch from the giant icebox,
the one we used to use for holidays,

    he doesn't like putting his stuff in other people's fridges
    but he likes his Coke really cold.
For you, he says, passing me a bright foil parcel
tightly wrapped. Inside sits

    a chunky cheese and pickle sandwich.

It's definitely not my favourite filling of all time,

    but today it is.

Saxophone

Dad tells me he would like to have been
    a jazz musician
if his mum and dad had let him
but he lived in Iran and boys like him
became doctors, lawyers, engineers;
they sneered at the artistic.
His dad went ballistic
when a guy on the street taught him
to play the saxophone,
like it was a dirty word
that should never be heard.

s*x*ph*n*!
slang, a high-pitched
musical moan,
a deep-seated groan,
the sound of being alone,
comforting, like home.

عشقت به دلم در آمد و شاد

Phone call

At nine o'clock, when we're slopped
in front of the TV, a phone goes off
and we both jump up. It's Dad's.
A number he doesn't recognise.

I better answer it, he says. *Hello?*

I know we're both thinking the same thing.
It must be the hospital, it must be about Mum,
no one else would call this late.

I watch Dad's face uncrumple
then stretch into a smile.

Ah, Mrs Hunter!
Sorry? No, no, not too late. Yes, yes, how can I —?
Oh?   No! The cat?! How did we —?
              You very sure? OK.
I come right away.

Dad hangs up,
claps one hand over his mouth.
What? I say. *What is it?*

> *We bloody trapped their cat under floorboard,*
> *that's what!*

Hysterics

We look at each other
     then in the next breath
          we burst out laughing,
               laughing
          laughing
the kind of laughter
          that crackles
                    and squeals
          like fireworks
     the kind that makes
your body shake
     twist, double up
          arch your back
     until we crash
onto the sofa
     with our laughter
          echoing above us
               like freed spirits.

A hundred quid

Late that night, when he gets in,
I hear Dad slipping
something under my door.
> My lights are off
> but I'm still awake.
It's an envelope, unnamed,
on the back Dad's irregular scrawl,
all the letters bent this way and that
like they're trying desperately to twist
into Farsi script.
> *Pay day, Azadeh!*
It's thick with folded banknotes,
ten pairs of Jane Austen's hooded eyes,
ten shy smiles.
I declare after all there is no
enjoyment like reading.

It's a fair point,
but a wad of tenners
does come pretty close.

Visit to Mum

We always joked that Mum's hands
had a life of their own,
they talked whenever she talked,
opening like buds
then twisting, threading, grasping,
clasping invisible words.

When I was little, I would watch them
like a puppet show,
forgetting to listen to the sounds
they were supposedly moving to.

Sometimes I'd grab one, suddenly,
to see if it stopped altogether
or if it writhed around like a fish,
but her other hand would quickly
release it from my grip
like a protective twin.

Now they lie still in her lap,
occasionally patting
the clothes that I chose for her
or trembling from the meds,
like a murmur.

Margaret's prescription

I've been listening to the playlist you made me,
Mum says with a weak smile.
It's lovely.
Not sure I understand it, mind.

You don't need to understand it, Mum.
It's just music.

Well, it feels a bit clever for me.
You understand it without even realising.
That's because you're a genius.

No, I'm not, Mum.

Don't know where you got it from, mind.
Certainly not from me. Your dad's family
always claimed they were related to royalty.
Maybe that's it.

Practising 'The Lark Ascending'

Andante sostenuto
    the speed of a summer evening breeze

pianissimo
    as quiet as rustling leaves

senza misura
    as free of time as bees

cadenza
    the chance to be as boastful as a blossoming tree

poco animato
    quietly alive, like a bird-swept sky

allargando
    widening, like a waking eye

largamente
    as broad as sunrise

quasi andante
  like creeping prey,
  sweet singing above, *cantabile*

poco meno mosso, then *allegro tranquillo,*
now *allegretto molto tranquillo!*

pianississimo
  as soft as a baby's sigh

lunga lunga
  hold on, hold on,
  the way a mother tries

fine
  let go, like the slinking tide.

Dad's at my door

I don't know how long
he's been standing there
on the landing   just out of sight.
I see his shadow, still
in the doorway.   Is he listening?

He never listens.
    He closes doors
      when it gets too loud
      or whenever I play scales
but he never *listens*.

I watch his shadow and suddenly
I stop, mid-phrase,
              when you'd least expect it.
He moves suddenly,
turns to the chest of drawers,
pretends to get a towel out.

I quickly start playing again
but with even more gusto,
producing my best vibrato,
making my bow
as clean as possible,
summoning everything in me
to keep him still
listening.

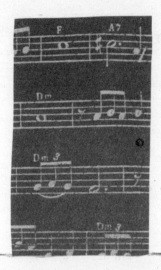

Googling

I google solutions for depression,
scroll through acronyms for therapies
CBT, IPT, MBCT, TLC,
adverts for medical centres, retreats,
dodgy home-made remedies,
then a million blogs
of top-ten depression-busting tips.

Eat healthily! Keep fit!
Get a good night's sleep!
Never underestimate
the importance of routine!

Then finally,
just as I'm about to give up,
I spot an article that looks like
it might actually
be useful.

Article on depression and creativity

When we *make*

we feel alive   we thrive

lose ourselves   pass time

mend and feel mended   contented

gardening   cooking   woodwork   whatever   functioning hands
make the mind flow

make creative thoughts grow   and so
we must daydream   nightdream   dream-dream!

Sing to our inner beings!

Wordsworth said poetry is

the spontaneous overflow of powerful feeling

all creation is   making order

out of disorder

a form of peace

a natural antidepressant

stilling the restlessness

within us

making us feel

that life   is
worth living.

Functioning hands

When I next visit Mum I pack her paints

and fancy watercolour pad, the ones we bought for

her birthday. I take her knitting bag too and her well-wrapped

packs of clay; place them on the shelf above her bed

without saying anything.

Practice with orchestra

I get to the church hall way too early,
before anybody else is there.
                        I circle it for a bit
then sit on a bench across the street,
spying on members of the orchestra
as they trickle in with their instruments.
                        They're all so *old*.
I'm definitely not going in until
I know Margaret's there.
                        Then I spot her
in her long, beige mackintosh and floral scarf,
striding towards the door, carrying
her bulging leather music case.

Relief and nerves suddenly
                        surge through me. I leap up
and scuttle over the zebra crossing,
slipping in right
behind her.

Getting ready

Margaret rubs my arm and winks.
Don't look so worried! she whispers.
                 But what if I make LOADS of mistakes?
It's the first rehearsal, it's FOR mistakes!
               I still can't get that double-stopping in tune.
But you will. Now get your violin out, dear.
We haven't got all day.

Nonetheless, I still take an age preparing my violin,
polishing the rosin dust off every little place
it shouldn't be, and even where it isn't,
until Margaret beckons me onto the stage.

She introduces me to the orchestra as her *star pupil*
and they smile at me kindly, like I'm a little child.
I try to smile back but I'm so nervous,
I've no idea if that's actually
what my face is doing.

Beating time

My
heartbeat
falls in step
with the rest
of the orchestra
until my pulse is
a metronome, measuring
the quavers, the semiquavers
the demisemiquavers and, just
about, the hemidemisemiquavers.
I'd warmed up my fingers that morning so
they mostly do what I tell them to; the shifts between
strings are pretty slick, but my double-stopping's *catastrophic!*

Proud

When we've finished our first run-through,
the lead violinist vigorously shakes my hand.
Bravo, bravo! he says, his hair flopping
with over-enthusiastic nodding.

I glance around and everyone's smiling
differently to before, like I've surprised them.
Margaret gives my shoulders a squeeze.
Wonderful, dear. You ought to be very pleased!

I pocket their smiles and words like gleaming coins,
photograph Margaret's beaming face in my mind.
Remember, remember this, I think,
when everything else goes to shit.

Kites

She
has not
touched the paints
but there is a pencil resting
on the pad, where she has started
tracing faint lines, the basic shapes of the room
hovering like ghosts on the page. I watch her hands on her
lap as she talks, willing them to soar, but
her sentences are short and
her fingers lift only
occasionally,
like kites
on a
qu
iet
b
r
e
e
z
e

Pheebs2005 has started an Instagram Live Story
Watch it now before it ends!

Hi guys and ladiiiiies!
So as you can see
Alicia and me
are a wee
bit tipsy
but good news
(yippeee!)
is that we
made you
COCKTAILS
so this is going to be
the best party
EVERRRRRRR!

I don't want to go

I don't want to remove every scrap of my body hair
and get half-naked without my make-up
in a summer bikini that's already too small,
that's all.

I don't want to turn up alone or too early or too late
and push through the crowd in Phoebe's house like a stranger,
looking for my best friend but also trying to
avoid her.

And all this, while thinking about my tiny tits,
the zits on my chin, my muffin-top hips,
and who is looking and who really
isn't.

Dad

I thought you were going out tonight, Dad says,
peering his head around the corner
as if the edge of my door is a guillotine.

> *You can come in, you know.*
> I slip my headphones off my ears
> so they sit around my neck, like a hug.
> *Just don't feel like it*, I shrug.

Isn't it Phoebe's party?

> *Yeah. But she doesn't need me there.*

Oh, he says.
*Well, maybe she doesn't need
but maybe she'd like you there.*

> I stare at him and realise it's probably
> the first piece of advice he's ever dared give me.
> *Whatever*, I say coolly.
> *I'm still not going.*

Five minutes later

And yes, I'm putting on a swimsuit
and slipping on a little black dress.
It's one Mum made for me last year
because every girl needs an LBD, she'd said.
I pile my thick dark hair on top of my head,
put on my big silver hoops,
a scoop of mascara,
dark red lip gloss,
and soon I'm as ready
as I'll ever be.

Birthday card

Phoebe always loves it
    when I make her birthday cards,
even though I can't draw for shit
    and she's the one studying art.

I cut out her favourite funky things,
    stuff she loves from magazines,
neon handbags, massive earrings
    and collage the number seventeen.

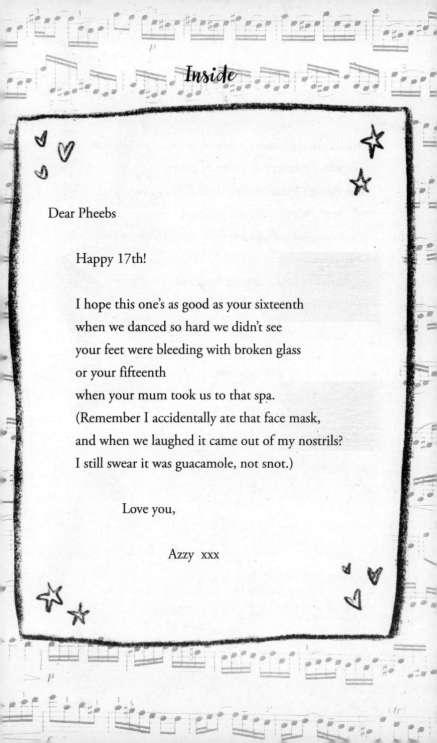

Inside

Dear Pheebs

Happy 17th!

I hope this one's as good as your sixteenth
when we danced so hard we didn't see
your feet were bleeding with broken glass
or your fifteenth
when your mum took us to that spa.
(Remember I accidentally ate that face mask,
and when we laughed it came out of my nostrils?
I still swear it was guacamole, not snot.)

Love you,

Azzy xxx

Arriving

I crunch up the gravel driveway to Phoebe's red front door,
worrying about who is going to answer it,
but *phew*, it's her older brother, Hugh,
looking blonder than ever.
He's on his second gap year, just back from Bali.

> *Alright, Az! Blimey, when did you grow up?*
> *Didn't you used to wear glasses?*

I don't tell him they're in my bag
and I can't see a bloody thing.
But at least my eyes look nice, right?

> *They're already in the pool.*
> *Go on through!*
> > *OK, cool.*

Cornered

AZZY! I suddenly hear Lottie scream.
I haven't seen you ALL TERM! How have you been?
I'm sorry I swapped studies with Alicia – she really
twisted my arm, you know what she's like.
I know you're not exactly
best buddies but she's alright, isn't she?! Now Azzy, tell me,
how are you REALLY doing, cos everyone's saying
you're being all weird and acting like some sort of recluse,
ignoring texts, fobbing off Phoebe with lame excuses.
I'm sorry, I'm pretty drunk and I'm probably
saying a lotta stuff I shouldn't, but you must already
know what everybody's saying, our school is basically
a village, without the poverty obvs, hey Azzy?!
Azzy?   AZZYYYYY?!
Where you GOING?!

Alicia

Oh thank God you're here, Alicia says,
stumbling towards me in her skimpy
tropical-print bikini which shows off all
her enviable curves. It's not exactly
the greeting I was expecting but something
surges inside me, pleased at being wanted
but worried by the serious look on her face,
her hands gripping my shoulders.

Why, where's Phoebe? I say. *She OK?*
Well, you wouldn't think it's her bloody birthday,
let's put it that way.
She's in her bathroom being a fucking misery.
She won't even talk to me.

You need to talk to her, Azzy.
Please.

288

Phoebe

Phoebe is scrolling through her phone,
hunched up on the marble floor,
her blue dress scrunched around her
like a crumpled flower.

Hey, I say, crouching down.

Thought you weren't coming, she mumbles. She frowns
at the screen some more, seemingly pretty drunk.

*I thought I wasn't either
but you can thank my dad.*

*Oh great, thanks, Az. You could at least pretend
you wanted to come.
I thought I was your best mate.*

You are.

Yeah, well, it doesn't feel like it.
You don't talk to me about shit
any more.
All that stuff with your mum,
you just shut me out.

        What about you?
        You're never around
        without Alicia glued to you.

I knew it! I knew you were jealous!

        Yeah, well, so what?
        So WHAT IF I AM?

Then I get up and slam the door

        before I scream

            the whole house

                down.

Drunk

I
hunt
for
the
drink,
which is
easy to find
because Phoebe
has a real bar, overlooking
the indoor pool and jacuzzi.
I start drooling spirits into a glass,
knocking them back, one by one,
desperately wanting to catch up
with everyone else's merriment.

And very soon, my head starts
to spin, my skin begins to thin
until I feel raw, like everything
inside me could pour
right
out.

Jamie

Hey, what you doing drinking alone?
It's Jamie. He's one of the only
guys who's fully dressed, except for his feet,
which are bare and slightly hairy – actually weirdly sweet.
He comes closer and the smell of him,
the warmth of his arms, his skin,
makes something in me stir
and suddenly we are kissing, urgently,
his stubble burning my lips and cheeks,
my hands on his muscled back, while his
drift down, caressing my curves.

> *Whoa, easy there, perv!* Alicia butts in.
> *Go get a room, lovebirds!*
> *Third floor is free.*

She winks at me, and Jamie is grinning
like the cat that's got the cream,
then suddenly, like a bad dream, I remember
> Mum
and this dark feeling surges in my stomach,
shivers through my veins like a ghost,
and I want to be small again
I want to be small again
ever so small.

Hey!

Where you going, Azadeh?
Come on,
we were having fun!
Please?
You can't just leave!

Az!
Az!

AZ!

Come back!

Shout out your heart!

Shout out your heart! Cry into the night sky,
let every single star hear you!
They're not just pretty, twinkling things,
up close they rage like fire, pyres of the universe.
      They have seen everything.

Shout out your heart! Sing the clouds electric,
see your lightning strike!
For forests will not burn and no one will die,
your anger shall light up the night
      like fireworks.

Shout out your heart! Spill your soul to the moon!
She will comfort you, she will
hold your sorrow in her fat belly
and slowly empty it into the galaxy
      until she thins to a crooked smile.

Shout out your heart! Let it break to pieces
and disappear into the air as dust,
sucked up by other people's lungs!
It won't be long before you grow a new one,
      then you'll remember love.

Phoebe

What the FUCK, Azzy?

Phoebe finds me
right at the bottom of her gigantic garden.

What's with the bloody shouting?
God, you're completely wasted.

I don't remember what happens next
but suddenly I'm crying and smearing mascara
all over her furry cream shrug
then we're hugging and Pheebs starts crying too.

> *Hey, why are YOU crying?* I say.

Because YOU are, you fool!
I'm sad for you!
That's what best friends do.

Promise

*Promise me that you'll never go
through anything like this alone
ever again.*

*Promise me that whenever you
are hurting, the first thing you'll do
is come to me.*

*Promise me that there is nothing
too shameful, too embarrassing
to share with me.*

*Promise me we'll
always be friends,
promise we can
always depend
on each other.*

Promise.

Happy birthday

Happy birthday,
by the way.

I made
you a card.

Phoebe starts to laugh.
*Wow, giant unicorn earrings
and matching heels!
Those actually exist?*

Apparently.

*Haha, it's . . . lovely.
Thank you.*

I missed you, you know?

I know.

I missed you too.

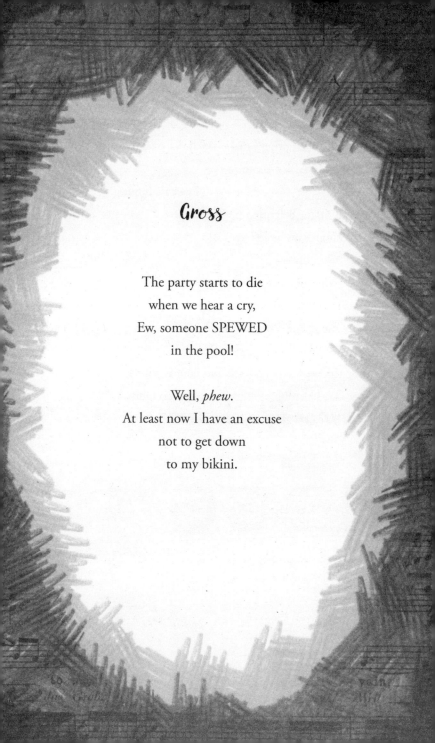

Gross

The party starts to die
when we hear a cry,
Ew, someone SPEWED
in the pool!

Well, *phew*.
At least now I have an excuse
not to get down
to my bikini.

After-party

We redo each other's make-up and see who's
crashed in which room.

                    I'm half-hoping
Jamie might be curled up somewhere
but Hugh says he left ages ago.

    God knows
      what he must think of me now.
Don't think about it! Alicia shouts
over the music. *Boys are shit!*
Look at Jay – he didn't even show!
She throws her head back and laughs wildly,
her face kaleidoscopic under the disco lights.
RIGHT! Let's get this party STARTED!

Hit it, DJ

We groove to Janelle Del Rey,
the bass at full max so it swells
deep inside us, and as the sea
does with sand, the beat pulls our bodies,
makes our muscles glide

                                slip

                                          slide

                          swerve

                  jerk

                      go absolutely

                                    BERSERK!

'Let the Music Take Over You'
feat. DJ Sorbet, Janelle Del Rey

It's our song! Phoebe shrieks,
pulling me closer to her.
Remember
Lower Fifth disco?!

'It's gonna be okaaaaaay,
I'll take your pain away!'

We scream the lyrics
at each other as if
we're raising spirits
from the dead.

'Oh, baby baby
come on an' move with me
yeah, come on an' groove with me
let the music take over you
let it do what it wants to do!'

We start to do the dance
as if our feet are in a trance
still possessing the memory
of all the obsessive hours we
spent watching the video
getting that swish of the toe
   just right
dancing, dancing all night
making everything
     alright.

Hangover

thick, fuzzy tongue
heavy, dizzy head
empty, churning stomach
think I might be

dead.

Hugh's fry-up

A heaven-sent smell
    which travels well
        on stale morning air,
        the meat-sweet caramel
            of apple and onion sausages,
                sizzling, crisp-edged eggs,
        golden, honey-roast bacon rashers,
squiggled and dashed
    with ketchup,
        and next to it
            a great big
                scoop of beans,
                    slopped on top
            of thick white toast,
        slathered most
        lavishly
            in butter.
              This
                  English
              dish
            is utter
        BLISS!

Phoebe's present

I nearly forgot,
I got you something.

WHAT? Two tickets for Janelle
DEL RAY!
WAHEY!!!
This must have cost you a bomb, Az!

Don't worry,
Dad gave me the money,
and anyway, I owe you practically
three years of coffees, remember?!

Truth

Phoebe asks me,

Where are you going now, Azzy?

I think about lying, saying
that Dad's phoned,
that I should get back home,
but I'm done with secrets now,
even in front of Alicia.

I'm going
to the hospital
to see my mum.

Oh shit, which one?
Alicia asks.

Phoebe starts to
tell her to shut up
but I interrupt.

It's OK.
It's Seaview Clinic, I say.

The psychiatric one.

Can we come too?

I promise we'll be
amazing company.

Journey

On the bus there, Alicia talks non-stop,
flicking through shit on her phone,
exploding with laughter every five minutes,
showing us some girl we don't know
and her ridiculous selfies.
Her noise is a relief
because me and Phoebe
are quiet the whole way there
until suddenly she puts her hand on mine.

I haven't seen your mum in months, have I?
Does she look the same?

Well, she's lost a lot of weight . . .
But other than that, she hasn't really changed, I say,
trying to reassure her.

Don't be nervous, Pheebs.
She'll be really pleased to see you.

Company

As we navigate the labyrinth
of hospital corridors,
patients shuffle past us,
some hooked onto nurses' arms
like strange umbrellas.
Phoebe looks straight on,
like Perseus passing gorgons,
clutching her handbag like a shield.
Alicia meanwhile looks around
as if she's in a museum,
everyone and everything an exhibit.
Hey, she says, skipping up the steps
to Mum's ward. *At least they've got
some decent vending machines!*

Gone

The nice nurse, Judy, is on duty.
I've brought some friends, hope that's OK?
> *Course it is, darling – boss is off today*
> *so I won't make them fill out no forms.*
She laughs heartily and rolls her eyes.
I roll mine too, then we walk on
down the hall towards Mum's room
number one-one-two.
Alicia hooks onto my arm,
Phoebe does the same,
and suddenly I feel safe.

The door is ajar, so I knock
then slowly push it open.
Mum?
She's not sitting on her bed as usual
and the sheets are tucked in so neat
it looks like no one's
slept in them.

I check the bathroom
but she's not in there either.

311

I hear myself breathing faster.

But Judy would've said if she'd
been moved
              or something had happened.
She would know.
                        I go back down the corridor
to ask her *Where's my mum?*
resisting the urge   to run.

Judy

I'm sorry, darling, I forgot she's gone to Arts 'n' Crafts
this morning! We just started this week, you see.
You know, I found her in her room, trying to shape
this big lump of clay, except she's got no tools!
And it got me thinking, why've we got no arty group?
We've got enough nurses into their knitting, scrapbooking and so on.
So we got a room, a few bits 'n' bobs, and now
everyone's wanting to come! And guess who signed up first?
     That's right, your mum!
She did the first one Monday and since then she's been
different, up and about, tidying her room, you'll see.
Go down that corridor, take a right
and you'll find her in the Lark Room, darling.

Mum

Mum is busy, head down, hands stretched like spiders
around a block of clay she's shaping into a bowl or vase.
Azadeh! she says when she eventually looks up.
She sounds pleased to see me but her eyes are swimming with worry.

You remember, Phoebe, Mum? She wanted to come with me.

Phoebe, yes, of course. Phoebe. Lovely to see you again.

And this is Alicia, Mum.

Hiya. Nice to meet you, Mrs Shaw.

Alicia. Nice to meet you too. I'm Kathy. You can call me Kathy.

OK

Your mum's well cool, Alicia says.
But then anyone who's got packets
of Jammie Dodgers stashed
in their cupboard
is good in my books.

> *She thought you were cool too,*
> *said you remind her of her sister.*
> *She was pretty wild.*

Glamorous too, I hope.

> *Er, nope.*
> *But you are, obvs.*

It was good to see her. Phoebe smiles.
She looks like she's doing OK.

> *Yeah, she's definitely*
> *better than she was.*

But what about you, Az?
You OK?

> *I think so.*
> *Or at least*
> *I will be.*

Uh-oh

I make the mistake of mentioning next week's concert.
Alicia shrieks, *OMG!!! CAN WE COME?*
I wanna see you doing your music geek thang.
We are SO coming, says Phoebe, *whether you like it*
or not. You better have a hot outfit.

Outfit? I haven't even thought about
what I'm going to wear!

I swear, you are SUCH A NERD, Alicia yells.
It's THE most important thing!
Right, that's it, girls. We are going

SHOPPING!

Shop till we drop

Alicia picks up all things leathery, leopard print, snakeskin.
There's no way I'm gettin' in THAT,
I say, as she throws me a spandex catsuit.

> *Oh go on, just for jokes, you'll look well cute.*

> *OMG you DO!* Pheebs squeals

> *Azzy, you look unREAL!*

Alicia dabs my lips with her bright red lip gloss.

> *There, now you look HOT.*
> *But we've gotta do something 'bout your mop.*
> *I know, let's get it CHOPPED!*

Absolutely NOT.

Sandy & Co.

Twenty minutes later and we're in this
fancy salon-spa in the posh part of town.
        Alicia's and Phoebe's mums go here all the time.
Alicia greets the owner like she's family.
SANDYYYYYYY!

        Alicia, BABE!

This sexy lady's been cutting my hair since I was six.
She's a freakin' genius.

Sandy's hair does look like
she's fresh off a Malibu beach.

Can you please please please
squeeze my friend in? Cut and blow-dry.

Panicked, I scan the place for a price list.
Hey, don't worry,
Alicia says as I check my purse.
I've got a freebie on my loyalty card.
It's ALL yours, girl!

Haircut

I watch Sandy in the mirror, all in black, moving swiftly
this way and that, like a hipster magician,
teasing my wet straggles with the teeth of her comb,
making thick straight-smooth strips
which she snips vertically and meticulously with
the tips of her scissors. Sometimes
she lifts strands high up in the air and cuts through
in one wild, diagonal swoop, her blade
sharp as a surfer descending a wave. And soon I am new,
frizz-free, split-end-free, mended,
with a tingling scalp, warm and red as a newborn's skin.
Shall we keep your curls or straighten?
Sandy asks. I glance at the other sleek heads in the salon.
I've always wanted straight hair
but then again . . .
Sandy sees
my hesitation.
Curls it is then.
Really? I say.
Defo! Straight's
so dull.
I'd love
to have hair
like yours!
But I'D
love
to have
hair
like
YOURS!

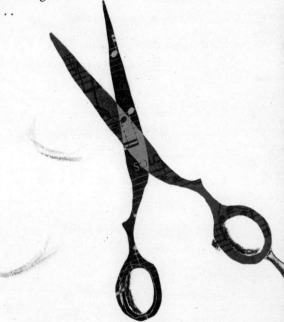

Shark ascending

I gotta go girls, sorry, I say
as we sip our Christmas caramel lattes.
I've got a practice for 'The Lark Ascending'.

The what?! they scoff.

'The Lark Ascending', the piece I'm playing.

'The SHARK Ascending'? Phoebe gasps.
*Whoah, that does sound cool. Is it all
DUUH-d' DUUH-d'
Like the music from* Jaws?

No – LARK, like the bird! Alica guffaws.
You're such a BIRDbrain, jeez!

And THAT is such a dad joke! laughs Pheebs.

Worst practice ever

Note to self,
when you have a hangover
do NOT surround yourself
with loud orchestral instruments

because every
                toot
                        trill
                pluck
                        plunk
                    hum
                chime
                        blare
                swell
I swear

is absolute

HELL.

Out

I'm going out, Dad mumbles
when he's finished doing the dishes.
Normally I just nod, but today I say

> *Don't you think it's odd*
> *that you never tell me where*
> *you're going?*

It's just a walk, fresh air,
it does me good.
I go the sea or woods.

> *Then you end up in the pub.*

Dad suddenly looks up,
frowning now.
Don't get cheeky
with me, young lady.
I'm not some drunk, you know.

I lower my head, watch him go,
feel the door
        slam   *between us.*

I run down the road

Wait for me, I say breathlessly.
You're not getting rid of me that easily.
I could do with some sea air too
and a drink. With you.

The Elgar Arms

We get Cherry Coke, cheesy crisps, a bottle of Becks
and drink to house rewires lined up for this month and the next.

We drink to cats trapped under floorboards being safe.
We drink to making up again with best mates.

We drink to my concert, to fear of stage fright.
We drink to you'll-be-better-than-alright-on-the-night.

We drink to Mum resurfacing, like driftwood on the sea.
We drink to tomorrow and getting our Christmas tree.

We drink to soon, to nearly, to hopefully, when
it'll be the three of us together, again.

Christmas tree

Dad
hauls home
a tree from down the road.
Mum usually
buys something tiny to fit our
living room
while I always beg to get one that's
big, as if
it would somehow make everything else seem big,
make us feel
more rich, and this year Dad gives in to me and gets this
enormous thing
that he has to cut the top off because it scrapes the ceiling.
We even have to buy
more decorations because it looks naked, and I choose them like I'm
buying diamonds
then hang each jewel on the tree ever so carefully, as if each one
is a quaver
a crotchet
a minim
hanging from a stave.

Hands

I've made you something.

You've made me something?

Mum has *made* me something.

Her *hands*
have made me
something!

And they've wrapped it
in crisp tissue paper,
tied it with thin pink ribbon
and given it to me.

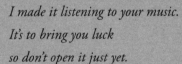

I made it listening to your music.
It's to bring you luck
so don't open it just yet.

Wait until your concert.

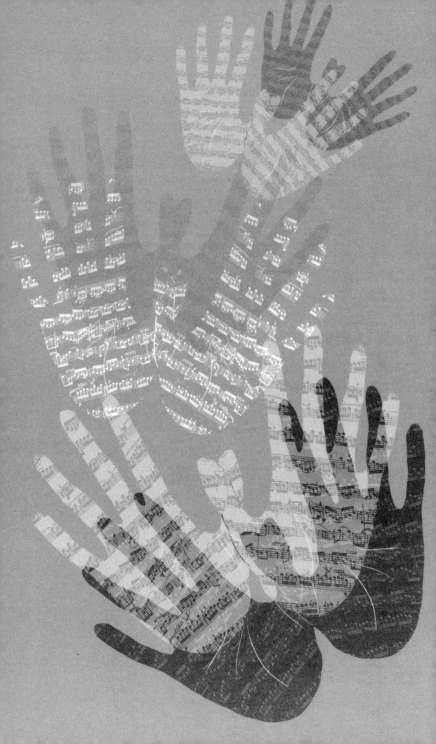

Getting dressed

I
put on
a long red dress
I got with Pheebs
and Alicia.
It clings
to my hips,
accentuates the colour
of my lips;
even my boobs
don't look too
bad in it.
I never think
of myself as fit
but for once
I can see
someone
you could
almost
call
pretty.

GOOD LUCK, AZZY! You're gonna be
bloody brilliant *starstruck emoji*
Remember it's the SHARK ascending, k?
Heheheh
Lots of love *heart times five*
GIF of a shark eating someone alive

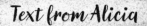

BREAK A LEG
you nerd,
I'm filming you
and 'gramming it
but hey no pressure,
whatever!

hashtag genius
hashtag prodigy
hashtag illbeyouragent
hashtag yourewelcome!

Peeking out

The auditorium is packed, full of hubbub,
snug with red felt, velvet, mahogany,
seats spiralling up to the ceiling,
where the lights are streaming
down like a hundred suns,
where every single one
of my notes will soon
be resounding.

Margaret's advice

Don't worry about
sweaty palms,
shaky arms,
making mistakes;

think about how
this piece makes you
feel
then make them keel
over with emotion,

just like you did
when you first
heard it.

Mum's gift

I nearly forget the package
 and unzip it from my bag,
  pulling the ribbon gently,
   unfolding the paper carefully,
    like reverse origami.
     White clay, smooth to the touch
      like eroded stone and
       etched with delicate feathers
      in the shape of tiny hearts.
    A bird! But not just any bird –
a beautiful soaring lark!

Showtime

I go up onto the stage with Margaret, striding confidently
the way Phoebe and Alicia taught me
in these heels, *little steps, heel toe, heel toe, sway, sway.*
We bow and the clapping quickly fades away
as if the audience are impatient for us to start.
We tune to the oboe's nasal parp,
first woodwind, brass then finally strings,
filling the room with that familiar, promising din.

East Wessex Orchestra's Christmas Concert
20th December
Soloist: Azadeh Shaw

Margaret grins at me then raises her arms like wings,
a puppet master with invisible strings,
lifting our instruments to mouths and chins,
solemn and ready to begin.
Clarinets, horns, strings, bassoon
begin to speak into the room,
two bars of three notes, lush and green,
immediately we can see the scene,
the hills and valleys, morning's prime,
the music of another time.
I enter with the voice of the lark,
softly trilling, bright yet dark,
wheeling up and down the strings,
my nimble fingers fluttering.
They all fall silent, listening,
then join my gleeful whistling,
a swelling sound that soars on air,
the kind that touches every hair,
every fibre of my being,
all-hearing, all-smelling, all-tasting, all-seeing.

After the last note . . .

there is a net of silence
stretched across the room
for a few seconds   and then
comes the thunderous roar of applause
like a crashing tide,
causing water to rise in me
and make my eyes shimmery.

I blink my tears away
and Margaret winks at me,
gestures for me to bow.
Now, I take in all the faces
shining back at me,
        Phoebe, Alicia, Miss Keats, Jamie . . .
        Jamie?
        Jamie came?!
I search through all the clapping hands
like a sea of butterflies
until finally I find
        Dad
and his hands, fluttering faster than anyone's
like they're about to take right off, pull
        his body off his seat   and onto the stage with me.

And then, and then, I see
who is sitting next to him, she
who strangely, I nearly
do not recognise,
because her eyes, her lips

   are smiling

and her hands are high in the air,
beating, beating, like drums

Mum
      Mum
            Mum

            my mum!

Epilogue
'Meditation' from Thaïs by Massenet

We are home
and the radio is on
in the kitchen
playing this piece
that is keeping us
warm indoors
while the April rain
dribbles down the window.

 It's that new one you play,
Mum says,
cutting clay teardrops
out of a lantern she's making.
She turns it upside down on the tray
and suddenly the falling tears
look like rising hearts.

 Beautiful music. Mum smiles.

Her eyes well
as the choir swells
underneath the violin.
It's an opera that ends in death,
a love realised too late,
lost faith   and yet,
the music transcends the pain,
frames it in a language that
takes our breath away,
saying,

Look, look at what keeps us alive
and what will survive of us!

Acknowledgements

There are several people I would like to thank for helping me start and (most challenging of all) finish this book:

My family and friends for all the love along the way, especially my first readers: Philippe Pereira, Bijan Sheibani and Casey Herbert.

Emily Talbot for all your support and excellent editing of various drafts. It would not have seen the light of day without you.

Jenny Jacoby for your sensitivity and sheer brilliance. I could not have wished for this book to be in better hands.

Talya Baker for your forensic eye and for tightening up the text so wonderfully.

Dominica Clements for designing the cover so beautifully.

Suzanne Cooper for doing wonders with my illustrations and text.

Jane Hammett for proofreading with the finest of fine toothcombs.

Molly Holt and the rest of the Hot Key team for bringing this book to its readers.

Elinor Cooper, Malachy Doyle, Kwame Alexander, Fiona Sampson, Elizabeth Acevedo and Celeste Rhoads for your guidance at various points in this journey.

Dr Monica Horovitz for your professional wisdom and encouragement.

Thank you to Dr. Carrie Baron for the article in Psychology Today (3/5/2012) *Creativity, Happiness and Your Own Two Hands*, which inspired the verse 'Article on Creativity and Depression'.

Finally, this book is in memory of two very special mentors: Mary Farmer and Dr Joanna Seldon.

Resources

If you are affected by any of the issues raised in this book, please consider reaching out to one of the organisations below.

Samaritans   Confidential emotional support for anyone in emotional distress, struggling to cope or at risk of suicide. Lines open 24/7. Call free on 116 123 or visit www.samaritans.org

Childline   A private and confidential service for young people up to age 19. Counsellors available to talk about anything. Call free on 0800 1111 or talk online at www.childline.org.uk

YoungMinds   Mental health support for young people, including a free 24/7 crisis text-messaging service. For urgent help, text 'YM' to 85258 or visit www.youngminds.org.uk

NSPCC   The UK's leading charity helping children. www.nspcc.org.uk

Mind   Provides advice and support to empower anyone experiencing a mental health problem and those who care for them. Infoline 0300 123 3393 or visit www.mind.org.uk

Thank you for choosing a Hot Key book.

If you want to know more about our authors
and what we publish, you can find us online.

You can start at our website

www.hotkeybooks.com

And you can also find us on:

We hope to see you soon!